The deputy turned toward Nugent, his eyes unable to focus for a moment as the image of huge Denzel Murdoch standing on the platform of the gallows stayed fixed in his mind. He could still hear Murdoch bellowing, "You'll be first, Marshal Bodine! Then I'm comin' after the rest of you!" The condemned man was still crying out his threat and naming his victims when the trapdoor opened and his feet plunged through the hole, breaking his neck.

Cold sweat beaded Lanny's face as he choked out, "Arnold, do you remember what Denzel said he would do to Sam when he came back from the grave?"

Nugent thought a moment, and then his face blanched. "Y-yeah. He . . . he said he would get Sam first. He said he would . . . climb out of his grave and . . . and bury Sam in it!"

Even as his words came from his mouth, Arnold Nugent's eyes bulged, and he recoiled as though he had been punched. Looking back at the fresh mound, he gasped, "Oh, dear God in heaven, no! Lanny, you don't think . . . it can't be!"

The Badge Series
Ask your bookseller for the books you have missed

THE BADGE: BOOK 8

★

THE STRANGER

★

Bill Reno

Created by the producers of
**Stagecoach, Wagons West,
White Indian,** and **Winning
the West.**

Book Creations Inc., Canaan, NY · Lyle Kenyon Engel, Founder

BANTAM BOOKS
TORONTO · NEW YORK · LONDON · SYDNEY · AUCKLAND

THE STRANGER

A Bantam Book / published by arrangement with
Book Creations, Inc.

Bantam edition / December 1988

Produced by Book Creations, Inc.
Lyle Kenyon Engel, Founder

ISBN 0-553-27621-2

Published simultaneously in the United States and Canada

Bantam Books are published by Bantam Books, a division of Bantam Doubleday Dell Publishing Group, Inc. Its trademark, consist-
ing of the words "Bantam Books" and the portrayal of a rooster, is
Registered in U.S. Patent and Trademark Office and in other
countries. Marca Registrada, Bantam Books, 666 Fifth Avenue,
New York, New York 10103.

PRINTED IN THE UNITED STATES OF AMERICA

KR   0 9 8 7 6 5 4 3 2 1

THE
STRANGER

★ BADGE ★

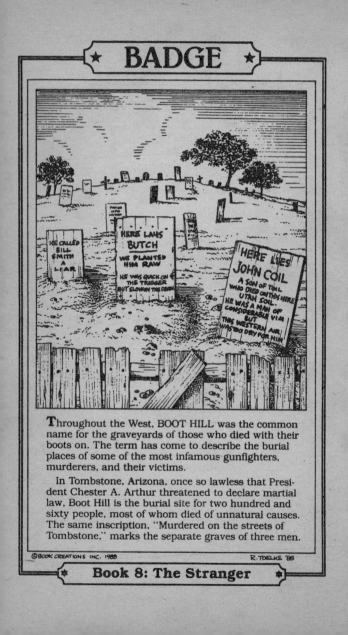

HE CALLED
BILL
SMITH
A
LIAR

HERE LAYS
BUTCH

WE PLANTED
HIM RAW

HE WAS QUICK ON
THE TRIGGER
BUT SLOWER'N THE OTHER

HERE LIES
JOHN COIL
A SON OF TOIL
WHO DIED ON THIS HERE
UTAH SOIL.
HE WAS A MAN OF
CONSIDERABLE VIM
BUT
THIS WESTERN AIR
WAS TOO DRY FOR HIM

Throughout the West, BOOT HILL was the common name for the graveyards of those who died with their boots on. The term has come to describe the burial places of some of the most infamous gunfighters, murderers, and their victims.

In Tombstone, Arizona, once so lawless that President Chester A. Arthur threatened to declare martial law, Boot Hill is the burial site for two hundred and sixty people, most of whom died of unnatural causes. The same inscription, "Murdered on the streets of Tombstone," marks the separate graves of three men.

©BOOK CREATIONS INC. 1988   R. TOELKE '88

❖ Book 8: The Stranger ❖

Chapter One

As the light from the rising sun penetrated his eyelids, he stirred awake, realizing that the hard, stony surface against which his back was pressed was the ground. Fighting the sensation that the ground beneath him was swelling, he rose up on his elbows and shook his head, only to have sharp pain stab his left temple and lights flash in his eyes like a shower of meteors. Then he became aware of a deep burning in his right side, and touching the area, he again experienced excruciating pain, and his fingers came away wet and sticky. He was bleeding.

When he realized that his teeth were clenched and his eyelids were pressed tight, he relaxed the muscles of his face. His right eye opened, but the other remained stubbornly shut. When he raised his left hand to find out why, his fingertips touched a mat of clotted blood. After gently peeling off the clot and opening the lid, he probed his face further, discovering a long, slender ridge burrowed along his temple and into his scalp. He knew immediately that a bullet had creased his head and that he had barely escaped death, but apparently he had been knocked unconscious by the powerful concussion of the bullet.

He looked around and saw that he was in a cemetery,

surrounded by dozens of granite and marble sentinels that glowed in the early-morning light. *I've got to get out of here,* he thought, pulling his legs up and rolling onto his knees.

Everything seemed to whirl, and he waited until the dizziness had subsided before attempting to stand. Sweat beaded his brow, and the cool morning wind seemed to freeze it on his skin. Nauseated, he swallowed against the acrid taste rising in his throat.

Closing his eyes to try to quell the sensation of movement, he became aware of several sounds nearby. One was the squeaking noise of wood against wood; the other was of several horses stamping restlessly. Turning his head slowly, he opened his eyes again to locate the source of the first noise.

A few yards away, at the head of a freshly dug grave, stood a weather-stained wooden marker, its crosspiece loose on the single nail. The two pieces of wood were rubbing against each other in the breeze. He started when he saw that near the fresh grave, sprawled amid several tombstones, were the bodies of three men.

Dragging himself a few feet to the nearest tombstone, he used it to steady himself. Slowly working his way to a standing position, he then saw the horses—three of them, all saddled—huddled by the entrance to the cemetery. Alongside the horses a rutted trail led out of the cemetery toward a road, and on the trail lay another horse, dead.

With trembling fingers he again checked the wound in his right side. It was bleeding slowly, but as far as he could tell, the bullet had passed through him.

Still light-headed, the man stood leaning against a gravestone for support and again let his eyes roam over the scene. There was no question he had been involved in a shoot-out . . . but why? And with whom? Were the three dead men his enemies or his friends? He searched his memory for answers but found none. In fact, he could not even remember how he got to the cemetery, or when . . . or for that matter anything beyond the few minutes since he had regained consciousness. Not a thing. Suddenly with a cold, numbing shock it hit him: He did not even know who he was.

Struggling to suppress the fear he felt welling up inside, the man tried to calm himself, telling himself that as soon as his head cleared, he would remember everything, and he began assessing his situation.

I was nearly killed by the bullet that creased my head. For some reason I was in a gunfight and—

He became aware that he was wearing a holster tied low on his right hip, and on the ground where he had been lying was a revolver. Kneeling carefully, grunting from the pain that the effort cost him, he worked his way to where the gun lay, picked it up, and looked at it. Somehow he knew that it was a Colt .45 Peacemaker, and that knowledge encouraged him. He was sure that the rest of his memory would soon return.

Opening the chamber, he found that five of the cartridges were spent. He automatically punched them out and reloaded the gun with cartridges from his gun belt, and then he slipped the weapon back into its holster.

Again using a gravestone to aid him, he slowly stood up and looked over at the dead men. He studied their faces carefully, but there was nothing familiar about them. However, judging from his original position and theirs, it was evident that he had shot it out with them. And he had apparently faced them alone, for if he had had a partner or partners, they would have done something to help him.

It dawned on him that he had not checked for any identification, and switching hands to stabilize himself against the tombstone, he rifled through his pockets, coming up with forty-three dollars in bills and two double eagle gold coins. There was also a small pocket-knife and the short stub of a pencil, but nothing more. Keenly disappointed, he took a deep breath, closing his eyes against a foggy wave of dizziness that briefly swept through him.

Looking beyond the cemetery, he saw that it was situated on top of a hill that overlooked a good-sized town a few miles to the east. Toward the south was a broad, sweeping valley with a river snaking its way through it and rimmed on both sides by rolling foothills giving way to mountains. Try as he might, the man could not make any of it seem familiar. It was all extremely disconcerting, and panic began rising in him again. Swaying as he clung to the tombstone, he asked himself, "Why can't I remember who I am, or where I am, or what I am doing here?"

A gust of wind suddenly rattled the crosspiece on the faded grave marker, making it squeak loudly, and the man's attention was drawn to it. Looking at it anew, he was struck by something that had not crossed his mind earlier. The wooden marker had seen its share of wind, rain, and snow, and although it was possible that the boards had been old and worn when they were nailed together, the paint that identified the name and death date of the grave's occupant was already faded. Yet despite the worn marker, the two-foot-high mound of dirt outlining the grave was newly turned. Squinting at the marker with curiosity, he read the faded inscription aloud:

Denzel Murdoch
Died
May 4, 1888

The wounded man tried hard to recall what the present date might be, but there was nothing, just that horrendous blank wall in his mind. Even his voice had sounded unfamiliar.

Pain seared his side again, and he knew the exertion had caused the wound to open up more. Looking down, he saw blood seeping through his shirt, and the crimson splotch was growing larger.

I've got to get into that town and find a doctor, he thought, *and I must do it now.*

Placing his right hand over the wound and pressing it tight in spite of the pain it produced, he slowly staggered toward the three horses standing outside the cemetery gate. As he weaved his way through the graveyard, recurring waves of dizziness made him frequently halt and hold on to the tombstones until he could safely move forward again.

Reaching the horses, he wondered if one of them was his, but none showed him any recognition. He figured from the droppings on the ground beneath them that they had been there for some time—probably since the previous evening—and he had no doubt been there just as long. He marveled that he had not bled to death already.

He chose the animal that stood closest to him, a young bay gelding. The horse bobbed its head and nickered, sidestepping as he reached for the saddle horn.

"Hold it, boy," he breathed. "I'm not going to hurt you. I just need your services for a while. You've got to get me into town."

The man's voice quieted the gelding, and it stood still while he gripped the pommel and strained to raise his left foot into the stirrup. A fiery streamer of pain shot through his side, and he felt a fresh surge of blood gush from his wound. He also felt light-headed, as though he were going to pass out, but clenching his teeth, he lifted himself up and eased his way into the saddle.

Urging the horse slowly along the wagon path toward the road, he managed to stay conscious by bending over in the saddle, keeping his head down. Watching the ground, something caught his attention: relatively fresh hoofprints along the path and beside them coagulated drops of blood. That meant someone else had been involved in the shoot-out, and although the man had been hit, he had still been able to mount a horse and ride away.

Without knowing why, his first instinct was to follow the trail of dried blood leading south, but he fought that irrational impulse. He had begun guiding the gelding toward the town when he heard familiar sounds—the rumble of hooves mingled with the metallic ring of harness and the rattle of a wagon. Lifting his head, he twisted in his saddle to see who was approaching. He had barely time to note that a buckboard carrying two men and a woman seated between them was heading his way when, as a result of his quick movement, dizziness overtook him again, descending like a curtain. He felt himself slipping from the saddle, and then everything went black.

Earlier that morning, when the gray light of dawn had come through her bedroom window at the Box B Ranch, some five miles west of Green River, Utah, twenty-three-year-old Bonnie Bodine sat up in her bed and looked across the room.

Stretching lazily, Bonnie, the only daughter of a prosperous rancher, threw her feet over the edge of the thick featherbed and then climbed down, padding across the room to her washstand, where she poured water from the large pitcher into a matching porcelain bowl and scrubbed her face, shocked into alertness by the cold water. Then she changed from her flannel nightgown into a simple cotton dress, buttoning the many tiny buttons that ran up the back, and slipped into her shoes. Sitting at her dressing table, she looked at her reflection in the mirror and brushed her long, honey-blond hair, twisting it into a knot and deftly pinning it into place with practiced fingers.

She tiptoed out into the hallway and descended the stairs of the still-quiet house. Since her mother had died three years previously, Bonnie was usually the first one to rise in the Bodine household, getting the fire started and breakfast cooking before her father and three brothers awoke. But as Bonnie neared the kitchen this morning, she smelled fresh coffee already brewed. She entered the high-ceilinged room to find her father sitting at the large kitchen table, a steaming cup of coffee in his hand.

Smiling warmly at him, the lovely blonde leaned over and kissed his cheek, saying, "Good morning, Daddy. Are you trying to take over my job?"

Looking up at his daughter with adoring eyes, Thomas Bodine returned the smile and replied, "Just in the coffee department, darlin'. I'll leave the cookin' to you."

As she touched his cheek tenderly, her gray-blue eyes studied his leathery face and she said, "Your color still doesn't look good to me. Maybe when the boys and I go into town, we should ask Doc Guthrie to ride out and check you over."

A large, beefy man standing over six feet tall and weighing about two hundred and thirty pounds, Thomas Bodine had not known a sick day in his life until his wife, Sarah, died. Since then, it seemed he often came down with one malady or another, and he looked considerably older than his fifty-nine years, especially since the little hair he had left was now completely white.

Grasping the small hand that touched his face, Thomas squeezed it and said, "There's nothing Doc can do, honey. I'll just rest a bit today, and then I'll be fine."

At that moment heavy boots thudded in the hallway, and three dark-haired young men filed into the kitchen and sat down at the table with their father. Bonnie watched her father's face as he looked affectionately at his sons. She was aware of how much Earl, just twenty-one, and Lamar, twenty-six, resembled their late mother and how much their father missed her. The two youngest sons were slender and stood just under six feet tall, while twenty-eight-year-old Frank, like his older brother, Sam, was tall and beefy like their father.

Thomas asked his sons, "What's on the agenda today, boys?"

"We've got some fence to mend over near the creek, Pa," answered Earl. "We'll do it after we get back from town."

"What're you goin' into town for?"

"Bonnie's runnin' low on pantry supplies, and we need to get some nails and lumber so we can fix up the shelves in the fruit cellar."

"And speaking of fixing," Bonnie put in, "I'm going to fix fried chicken tonight, and I'd like to invite Sam to come and eat with us."

She watched Frank from the corner of her eye as Sam's name was brought into the discussion. Bad blood had developed between the two elder brothers, and it was a grief to the old man. Just over a year earlier, Frank had fallen in love with a Green River woman and proposed marriage, but Sam had fallen in love with her, too. The resulting triangle ended in a bloody fistfight, and even though the woman turned from both of them and married another man, Sam and Frank had hardly spoken since the incident. Frank seemed to be carrying the grudge more than Sam was, although he usually denied that it was his stubbornness that kept the feud alive.

Noting the sour look on Frank's face, Thomas Bodine inquired, "Frank, are you goin' into town with the boys and Bonnie?"

Shaking his head, Frank replied, "No, Pa. I'll just stick close to home, since you're not feelin' too well. Besides, there's some work that needs to be done on that broken step on the back porch. I'll fix it while everyone's gone."

"We can do that after we repair the fence, Frank," offered Earl. "Why don't you come with us? Pa will be all right, won't you, Pa?"

Frank's mouth turned down and his eyes glistened with malice. Not giving his father a chance to comment, he blurted, "I'm really not interested in goin' to town, little brother. Let's just leave it at that, okay?"

The atmosphere around the table tensed, and seeking to ease it, Bonnie spoke up and said, "Frank, I'm going to make blackberry pies, since I know they're your favorite kind. You *will* eat with us tonight, even if Sam is here, won't you?"

Since their fight had taken place, Frank nearly always managed to avoid eating with the family when his older brother was present. But he had a warm spot in his heart for his little sister, and giving her a faint grin, he nodded, "Sure, little one. How can I refuse with such an incentive?"

A smile had worked its way across Thomas Bodine's wide face. "That's what I like to hear, son! You and Sam need to bury the hatchet and—"

"Don't misunderstand, Pa," Frank cut in. "Just because I'll be sittin' at the same table with Sam doesn't mean he and I are gonna do any huggin' and kissin'. Jane was in love with me, and Sam knew it. He jumped in and proposed to her and muddied the waters. She and I would have been happily married today if Sam had backed off like he should have done. I'll tolerate his presence for the sake of the family, but *tolerate* is all I'll do."

Sighing, Thomas Bodine said no more.

After finishing a few chores, Earl and Lamar Bodine placed their sister between them on the buckboard seat to travel into Green River, and it was nearing eight-thirty when they approached Cemetery Hill.

Still thinking about the feud between Sam and Frank, Bonnie said to her brothers, "I wish there was something I could do to help them settle their differences. Their battling isn't doing Daddy's health any good."

"That's for sure," agreed Earl. "He doesn't need the kind of strain it's putting on him."

"Maybe if it was laid out before them just like that, they'd settle it for Pa's sake," said Lamar.

Bonnie sighed. "It'd be worth a try. Maybe one of us can get the two of them together tonight after supper and somehow make them see that their fight is hurting all of us. The problem will be to get them to stand still long enough in each other's presence to listen."

Earl looked at Bonnie. "If anybody can do it, big sister, it'll be you."

"Yeah, Earl's right. Those big lummoxes will do anything you ask them to do—you know that."

Bonnie shrugged and agreed, "Okay, boys. I'll do my level best to—" Her attention was caught by a man riding bent over in his saddle, and she pointed at him, saying, "Look! That man on his horse—he seems to be sick or something. Oh, he's falling off!"

Earl Bodine snapped the reins and shouted at the team, urging them toward the spot where the rider lay in the road beside his horse. Moments later the wagon skidded to a halt in a cloud of dust, and the three Bodines hopped down from the wagon and knelt beside the unconscious man.

Giving him a quick examination, Bonnie observed, "I think he's been shot a couple of times. From the looks of that bloody crease on his forehead, I'd say he's plenty lucky to be alive." She looked up at her brothers and ordered, "Lay him on the bed of the wagon, and I'll see what I can do to stop the bleeding in his side. Then we'll need to get him to Doc Guthrie as quickly as possible."

Earl nodded and stood up. He was walking to the rear of the wagon to let down the tailgate when his attention was drawn to the dead horse lying on the wagon trail that led into the cemetery. Looking farther, he saw two horses standing near the cemetery gate and the bodies of three men lying among the tombstones. Swearing softly, he said, "Look over there! The cemetery looks more like a battlefield!"

Bonnie and Lamar followed their brother's pointing finger and took in the grisly scene before them. Shaking her head in disbelief, Bonnie suggested, "Let's get this man into the wagon so I can work on him, and while I'm doing that, you two had better check on those others."

The two brothers lifted the unconscious man and gently carried him to the wagon, and then Bonnie climbed in and knelt next to him, carefully unbuttoning his bloody shirt to expose the wound. Examining him, she saw that the bullet had passed through his body about an inch in from his side. She lifted the hem of her dress and tore off a long strip of petticoat for a makeshift bandage, pressing it to the wound and stemming the flow of blood. Using another length of petticoat, she secured it.

The young woman examined the bullet crease on the man's left temple and was pleased to see that the blood there was clotted and dried, indicating that the wound was already healing.

Having done all she could, she took a moment to look the man over. She estimated that he was about thirty years of age and six feet tall. He was slender yet muscular, and he appeared to have been in excellent physical condition before being shot. Bonnie decided that his health had probably helped toward keeping him alive with such a serious wound. Looking again at his face, she found his angular features quite handsome, as was his dark brown, wavy hair. It was well trimmed, and his face was clean-shaven. Idly she speculated about the color of his eyes.

Turning her head, she looked over to where her brothers were walking among the tombstones and grave markers. She watched as they knelt down and examined the three bodies. Picking up the dead men's guns, they walked to another spot a few yards away, knelt again briefly, and then stood up, looking back at the wagon. Bonnie guessed that they had found the spot where the injured man had been shot—probably by one or more of the three men. She hoped he would be able to tell her what happened when he regained consciousness—and she also found herself hoping that his being shot had not been justified.

Suddenly the man began to roll his head and lick his lips. She turned back to him as a moan came from his throat and his eyelids began to flutter. Leaning over him, she pushed the hair back from his forehead and then waited for him to regain consciousness.

As he opened his eyes, a spasm of pain shot through his head. Struggling to make out the features of the person leaning over him, he vaguely remembered the wagon that he had seen coming toward him before everything went black. There had been a woman on the wagon seat between two men, and he realized he was now in the bed of that wagon. As his vision cleared, he saw that the woman looking down at him had honey-blond hair, which framed a beautiful face, and that her gray-blue eyes were warm and inviting. It was the same woman he had seen in the wagon.

"Hello," the young woman said softly. "I'm glad to see you're awake. My name is Bonnie Bodine. My brothers and I reached you just after you fell from your horse. Right now they're checking on three men lying over there in the cemetery, but then we'll take you into town to the doctor. I've bandaged the wound in your side as best I could, but you need proper medical attention. I'm afraid the other three men are dead."

Running his tongue over his dry lips, the man said, "I . . . I really appreciate . . . your kindness. Is the wound in my side pretty bad?"

"You were very lucky because the bullet passed on through," she responded, "but I think you've lost a lot of blood, although I have it pretty well stopped for now." Lifting her eyes toward the cemetery, she told the man, "My brothers are coming back now. The ride into town will be bumpy, but it's only a couple of miles."

"What . . . what's the name of the town?" he asked.

Looking somewhat surprised, she replied, "Green River."

"Green River? Green River *where*?"

"Utah." Cocking her head sideways and squinting, she asked, "You don't know where you are?"

"No, ma'am," he said. "I . . . I can't seem to remember very much at all. I—"

"What's your name?" she asked.

He looked at her helplessly. "I don't know."

"You . . . you don't know your name?"

"No. As a matter of fact, I have no idea where I'm from or what I'm doing here. My memory is completely blank beyond waking up in the cemetery, getting on that horse, then passing out again."

Bonnie's hand went to her mouth. "You have amnesia. It must be from the bullet that clipped your head. I'm sure—"

"Bonnie!" Both of her brothers gasped out her name simultaneously as they ran up to the buckboard, breathing hard.

Her head came up.

"Somebody's been messin' around with Denzel Murdoch's grave!" Lamar declared.

Bonnie Bodine's face lost color at his words. "What do you mean?" she asked, eyes wide.

"It's been dug up!"

Staring at her other brother, she said, "Earl, what is he talking about?"

Earl rubbed a nervous hand over his mouth and replied, "Denzel's grave looks like a new one. I mean, the dirt is newly turned and in a mound like it was dug yesterday."

"But that's preposterous!" she exclaimed. "You must be mistaken. Somebody must have moved the grave marker from Denzel's grave and put it at the new one as a joke."

"That's what I thought at first," he told her, "but it's Denzel's grave, all right—smack-dab between Clara Otis and Brent Harrison, just where it's been for the past eleven months."

The man in the wagon could tell that the Bodines were badly shaken. He could see that something about this Denzel Murdoch frightened them—something more than someone's having tampered with his grave.

With a tremor in her voice Bonnie said, "Let's get into town and tell Sam. We need to get this man to Doc Guthrie quickly, too."

Earl and Lamar climbed onto the wagon seat, Lamar picking up the reins, while Bonnie stayed in the bed beside the stranger. Looking up at her from his supine position, he said, "Who is Sam?"

"He's the town marshal. He's also our oldest brother."

The wagon started off with a slight lurch, and then it stopped just as suddenly. Lamar touched Earl's arm and said, "We can't just leave this man's bay out here. I'll go tie it to the back of the wagon."

"What about the other two horses?" Earl asked.

"We can send someone from the livery back for them." Then turning on the seat, Lamar declared, "Here, this must be yours, mister," and he handed the wounded man a gray felt hat that he had found in the graveyard.

The hat did not look familiar to him, but it was not surprising; nothing else did, either. The thought passed through his mind that he did not even know what he looked like, and he was sure he would not know his own face if he saw it in a photograph. Panic started to rise within him again, but it subsided when he looked up into Bonnie Bodine's face. There was something about her that caused a gentle peace to settle over him.

While Lamar Bodine tied the gelding to the back of the wagon, he smiled at the wounded man and said, "Where you from, pardner?"

"He doesn't know," Bonnie answered for him.

Earl twisted around on the wagon seat, his brow furrowed, and at the same time Lamar looked at his sister askance and said, "Huh?"

"The bullet that creased his head must have given him amnesia. He can't remember his name, either."

"What *do* you remember, stranger?" queried Earl.

"I can't recall anything other than waking up early this morning and finding myself bleeding."

Lamar shook his head and started to say something when he heard the rumbling sound of galloping horses, and he and the others looked toward the east. A band of eleven riders came thundering up to them and drew to a halt, the dust cloud that surrounded them slowly drifting away as the leader—a tall, thin man in his late thirties wearing a town marshal's badge—eyed the wounded man lying in the bed of the wagon.

"Howdy," he said to the Bodines. "I'm Keith Marksberry, marshal of Crescent Junction."

"We know of you, Marshal," Bonnie said amiably. "And we've made the twenty-mile trip to Crescent Junction quite a few times."

"I'm Lamar Bodine," spoke up the older of the two brothers. "This is my sister, Bonnie, and my brother, Earl."

"Bodine?" said Marksberry. "Any relation to Green River's marshal?"

Nodding, Earl said, "Yes, sir. Sam's our oldest brother."

"Fine man," declared Marksberry. Then, staring at the wounded man in the wagon, he asked, "Some kind of trouble?"

"Shoot-out," volunteered Earl. "This man is the only one who survived it."

"Shoot-out?" Marksberry's eyebrows arched. "Where are the dead ones?"

Gesturing with his chin, Earl replied, "Over there in the cemetery. There are three of them."

While the other riders looked toward the graveyard, Lamar asked, "Is this a posse, Marshal?"

"Yeah," Marksberry answered as he dismounted, still staring at the wounded man. "We're trailing five men who robbed the Crescent Junction Bank late yesterday afternoon. They killed a customer inside the bank and wounded my deputy as they were riding away. We want them real bad."

The wounded man in the wagon felt the weight of Marksberry's stern glare, but Lamar Bodine came to his rescue, saying quickly, "We saw this man fall from his horse, unconscious. My sister bandaged the bullet wound in his side so he wouldn't bleed to death on the way into town to see the doctor. But he can't seem to recall—"

Lamar's words were cut off by one of the possemen calling to Marksberry, "Marshal, looks to me like there was another survivor to the gunfight, and he seems to have headed south." The man was leaning from his saddle, looking at the trail of dried blood that led from the cemetery and out onto the road.

Marksberry walked over and checked it out himself, and then he returned to the Bodine wagon and re-garded the wounded man coldly. Narrowing his ice-blue eyes, he said, "Three and two makes five."

The implication of what the lawman was saying seemed to strike Bonnie Bodine like a blow in the stomach. She blinked, looked at Marksberry's weathered face with consternation, then stared at the stranger. The wounded man read the disbelief in her eyes, as though she was reluctant to accept the marshal's assessment of the situation.

Leaning over the wagon bed, Marksberry slipped the Colt .45 from the wounded man's holster and said, "Now, why don't you just tell me all about it, mister?"

"I can't, Marshal," he replied.

"What do you mean you can't?" Marksberry grunted.

"I have no memory of *anything*."

"You're saying you've got amnesia or something?"

"I guess so," the stranger said, nodding.

The lawman's features reddened with anger. "I've had a lot of your kind pull plenty of bold-face lies out of nowhere, mister," he said disgustedly, "but you're the first to come up with this one."

Bonnie Bodine stiffened. "He's not lying, Marshal Marksberry," she said in a crusty, defensive tone. "Take a look at the left side of his head where a bullet came within a hairsbreadth of killing him. Is it so hard for you to believe that the concussion of the bullet might have jolted his brain and robbed him of his memory?"

Marksberry leaned down close and examined the bloody furrow that the bullet had plowed in the man's left temple. Straightening up, he replied, "I suppose it's possible, Miss Bodine—but it's also highly improbable."

The blonde's lips tightened and her eyes narrowed as the lawman gestured to two of his men and said, "Come with me. I want to take a gander at the three dead ones. The rest of you stay here and make sure our wounded friend doesn't get any ideas about trying to make a run for it."

As Marksberry and the two men headed for the cemetery, Bonnie snapped at the marshal's retreating back, "This man couldn't even get into a saddle, much less make a run for it!"

The stranger smiled up at her and said softly, "Thank you for your confidence, Miss Bodine. You've got more than I have."

"You're no outlaw," she said stubbornly. "I just know it."

"I hope you're right," he mused.

Tearing her gaze away from his, she looked at the men of the posse and declared, "We've got to get him to Doc Guthrie right away. He's lost a lot of blood."

"I'm sure the marshal will agree with you, miss," said

one of them, watching her admiringly, "as soon as he returns."

In the cemetery Keith Marksberry examined the three dead men. Looking them over carefully, he said to his men, "Two of them I don't recognize, but the one in the middle is Curly Stoddard, a known bank robber and killer. I've got a wanted poster on him in my office, and I received a bulletin from the U.S. marshal's office in Salt Lake about three weeks ago that said Stoddard was in our area, leading a gang of bank robbers."

"Sounds like the bird in the wagon is trying to put one over on us, Marshal," commented a member of the posse.

Marksberry did not comment on the man's remark. He was too busy examining a blood-soaked piece of ground a few yards from a fresh grave. Looking repeatedly between the three dead men and the bloodied ground, he called to his men, "It appears that there was some kind of dispute between the members of the gang, and they decided to settle it with lead."

His two men nodded their agreement.

Walking over to them, Marksberry said, "Let's check the saddlebags on those two horses and see if any of the bank's money is in them."

While the possemen searched the two horses to learn what they were carrying, the marshal did the same to the bay tied to the rear of the Bodine's wagon. None of the saddlebags contained bank money.

Walking around the wagon, Marksberry asked the wounded man, "Was it you or the guy who rode away that left a gallon of blood near that fresh grave up there?"

"It must've been me," said the stranger. "That's where I was lying when I woke up."

"Marshal," interjected Bonnie, "we've got to get him to the doctor now. If you need to question him further, can't you do it in town?"

"We'll head for town in a minute, Miss Bodine," the lawman said evenly. Peering intently at the wounded man, he queried, "You fellas have a fight over the loot from the bank robbery?"

"I don't have any idea," responded the stranger. "I'm telling you the truth about my loss of memory. I don't know who I am, Marshal, nor do I know where I'm from or why I'm in this particular place. But there's something in me that says I'm not an outlaw."

"There something in me that agrees with him," Bonnie declared intently, glaring at Marksberry.

"The evidence is against you, mister," growled the lawman. "There were five men who robbed our bank yesterday—three bank employees and two customers all attested to that. There are three dead men up there in the cemetery. One other rode away, leaving a bloody trail. That's four, in case you've forgotten how to add, too, and you make number five. Now, if you were in my boots, how would it stack up to you?"

The stranger's voice was resigned. "I'd come to the same conclusion that you have, Marshal."

Smirking, the marshal said, "Let me refresh your memory some more, fella. The leader of your gang was Curly Stoddard, one of the dead ones up there. Now, I want to know your name and the name of the one that got away."

"Look, Marshal," Bonnie interrupted, "we're going to have another dead man on our hands if we don't get him to Doc Guthrie. You and your posse can follow us to town, but we're going right now—even if I have to drive this wagon over you and your men!"

"All right, all right," Marksberry said with a sigh. "We'll follow you."

Just before the wagon started up, the marshal eyed the wounded man again and said, "I'm going to put you under the doctor's care in the custody of Marshal Sam Bodine, mister. Then these men and I are going after your fellow gang member, the one who rode away.

When we catch him, we'll take him back to Crescent Junction to stand trial—just like you'll be doing the minute you're well enough. As soon as the witnesses to the bank robbery get up on the stand and identify you, maybe you'll give up this amnesia cock-and-bull and decide to tell the truth."

"I *am* telling the truth," the stranger said flatly.

"You may have to eat your words, Marshal," Bonnie said angrily. "Maybe this man is a law-abiding citizen who just happened to run into the robbers and had to fight it out with them to protect himself. Maybe the fifth robber got away, too."

Looking at her smugly, Marksberry said, "I've been in this business for nine years, miss, and I assure you I know about outlaws. This man is as guilty as sin."

"I say you're wrong," declared the blond woman.

"We'll see," the marshal said as he turned toward his horse.

As the buckboard rolled toward Green River, followed by the posse, the stranger looked up at Bonnie Bodine and smiled at her—and not just out of gratitude. Though he could not remember anything about his past, he was absolutely certain that she was the most captivating woman he had ever met.

Chapter Two

The Bodine wagon traveled along Green River's main street, followed by Marshal Keith Marksberry and his ten riders. As the procession headed toward Dr. Walter Guthrie's office and clinic, it drew the attention of the many passersby.

Immediately after the wagon halted in front of Doc Guthrie's large three-storied house, Bonnie sprang down and dashed into the office to prepare the way for the wounded man.

Looking up at the sound of her footsteps, the aging, silver-haired physician put down the thick medical book he had been reading and peered over his spectacles at Bonnie. "Well, if it isn't my favorite country girl. How's your father doing?" he asked with a smile.

"Not too badly, Dr. Guthrie, although I'm here for another reason entirely."

"Oh?" said Guthrie, removing his glasses and standing up.

Bonnie quickly told him about finding the wounded man by the cemetery and of the gunfight that had apparently taken place. She had just finished explaining that the stranger had amnesia when the door opened and the Bodine brothers entered, carrying the handsome stranger, with Marshal Keith Marksberry on their heels.

Guthrie led them from the office to a much larger room, which served as his clinic and surgery and smelled of medicines. Against one wall were glass-fronted cabinets, and oak cupboards and a washbasin were arrayed on the other walls. In the center of the brightly lit room was a waist-high table where the doctor performed examinations and operations.

Pointing to the table in the center, he said, "Lay him right there, men."

After the wounded man was placed on the table, Guthrie did a quick examination and mumbled something to himself. Turning to the petite blonde, he said, "Bonnie, would you go into the house and tell Bertha I need her help? This wound has to be cleaned out and stitched up quickly, and it'll be best if we administer some ether to anesthetize this man."

Bonnie nodded and disappeared through the door that led to the servants' quarters, where Bertha Nash, Guthrie's housekeeper and medical assistant, resided.

Guthrie, turning to the Bodine brothers and Keith Marksberry, said, "I'll need you gentlemen to step outside. If you're of a mind to stay around, please do so in the waiting room."

"I don't think you understand, Doctor," Marksberry said roughly. "This man is an outlaw, and I've put him under arrest. Until I can get Sam Bodine here to keep an eye on him, I'm not budging from this room."

Regarding the lawman with piercing dark eyes, Guthrie said, "From what Bonnie just told me, you don't know for certain that this man is an outlaw."

"Female sentimentality," Marksberry countered with a sarcastic sneer.

Guthrie noticed Earl Bodine stiffen, but the young man held his peace as the physician snapped back, "I've known Bonnie since she drew her first breath, Marshal. The girl's got good horse sense as well as being an excellent judge of character, and since she feels very strongly that this man wasn't part of the gang, I'm inclined to go along with her."

"Until there is proof to the contrary," Marksberry rasped, "this man will stay in custody. I'm going to put him in Marshal Bodine's care until I return."

"I don't have time to stand here and argue, Marshal," Guthrie said huffily. "This wound has got to be tended to immediately. Besides, this man couldn't run away if he wanted to. Now, you go find Sam if that's your pleasure. Just don't let the door slam into your backside on the way out."

Lamar touched Earl on the shoulder, and the two of them followed Keith Marksberry out the door. Over his shoulder, Lamar said, "Doc, tell Bonnie we'll see her in a little while, when we come back with Sam."

The silver-haired physician nodded and got to work. As he removed the wounded man's shirt he commented, "So you don't remember a thing, Bonnie tells me."

"That's right," said the stranger. "Everything's a total blank."

"Well, you're about to experience even more of a blank. I'm going to administer some ether to put you under while I work on that wound. It'd be mighty painful, otherwise."

"Thanks, Doc. I appreciate your taking such good care of me."

"That's my job, son."

At that moment Bonnie returned, saying, "Bertha will be here shortly, Dr. Guthrie."

"Good. While we're waiting, why don't you wheel my instrument table over here for me, and I'll wash up."

While Bonnie did as she was asked, Guthrie went to the washbasin and primed the pump, filling the basin with water and washing his hands with lye soap.

The doctor was just finishing when the door to the clinic swung open and a large woman in her late fifties, clad in a white cotton dress, came through the door, propelling herself in a wheelchair.

"Ah, good, Bertha," the physician exclaimed. "Just in

time. This young fellow needs our help, so let's get to work, shall we?"

The big woman had a gentle and warm way about her that immediately put Guthrie's patients at ease. After the first startling impression, people seldom noticed the heavy powder and lip paint she always wore in a futile attempt to improve her fleshy, homely face.

Speaking in a deep, throaty voice, she said, "Now, young man, you can just relax because Doc Guthrie is the best, and he'll fix you up good as new."

"I don't doubt it," the stranger said, and he smiled at her. "Miss Bodine brought me to him, and if he has her confidence, that's good enough for me."

The blond woman smiled warmly at him.

Watching her face carefully, Dr. Guthrie said, "Bonnie, you can stay in here if you won't find the surgery too upsetting. By the way, your brothers said they'd see you when they return with Sam."

"Thank you, Doc," Bonnie said. "I'd like to stay."

Guthrie had Bertha administer the ether, and within seconds the physician was able to begin swabbing the wound, probing carefully to make sure nothing was damaged.

"This sure beats the old days," he commented to the two women. "Not long ago this young fellow would've been biting down on a bullet to keep from screaming while I did this. Now he doesn't feel a thing, and when he wakes up, it'll all be over."

After leaving two of the possemen as guards on Doc Guthrie's porch, Crescent Junction's marshal walked up the street with the Bodine brothers to find their brother Sam, the town marshal of Green River.

When the three men reached the marshal's office, Lamar Bodine opened the door and entered first, smiling in greeting at a lanky young man in his early twenties seated behind the desk.

Deputy Lanny Hughes smiled in return, easing back

in his chair as he said, "Good mornin', Lamar, Earl. Well, I'll be, if it isn't Keith Marksberry. What brings you to our fair town? Are you all together or did you just follow these two Bodines in through the door?"

The marshal shook hands with the deputy and replied, "I'm with these fellows, in a manner of speaking. I wish I could say it was something pleasant that brings me here, Lanny, but it's not. Our bank was robbed late yesterday afternoon. My posse and I tracked the robbers this way and found all but one of them up in the cemetery."

"The cemetery?"

"Yeah. There were five men in the gang, and three of them are lying up there dead. They must have had some kind of a disagreement among themselves; it turned into a gunfight. One of them got away, although he left a trail of blood that shows he's headed south. The Bodines, here, found the other one all shot up. He's being tended to by Dr. Guthrie, but when the doc's finished, I'll need to leave him in Sam's custody. Is he around?"

Lanny Hughes shook his head. "Nope. Sam hasn't come to the office yet this mornin'. I expect him to be showin' up just about any minute."

Earl Bodine turned to his brother and said, "We'd better go on over to Sam's house. We've got to tell him about the grave, too."

"Grave? What do you mean?" The deputy looked puzzled.

"There's something strange at the cemetery," Earl replied. "Somebody's been messing with Denzel Murdoch's grave."

Lanny puckered his brow. "How's it been messed with?"

"It's like they dug it up, then filled it in again."

The deputy's face went white.

"You got some crazy grave robber on the loose?" asked Marksberry, noting Lanny Hughes's reaction.

"Grave robbers don't bother to fill the graves back in when they steal a body," said Earl. "No, it's something really weird."

Still pale, Lanny Hughes half whispered, "If it was any other grave—"

"Yeah, I know," agreed Earl. "Well, come on, Lamar, let's get over to Sam's place." Heading for the door, he said to Marksberry, "You might as well wait here, Marshal. We'll be back with Sam shortly."

"I'll go with you. I need the marshal to get to the clinic as soon as possible so my posse and I can get on the trail of the robber that's still loose."

"I'll go along, too," put in Lanny. "I want to go to the cemetery with Sam."

Walking briskly, the four men turned off Green River's main street and headed for Sam Bodine's house, which was on a side street less than three blocks away. As they hurried along, Marksberry, curious to know why the deputy seemed so frightened, asked what the significance of the grave was.

Earl and Lamar looked at each other, but they said nothing.

Pressing for an answer, Marksberry said to Lanny Hughes, "Well, Deputy, are you going to fill me in on this—what was the name—Denzel Murdoch?"

Looking reluctant to discuss it, Lanny shrugged off the question, saying, "Oh, it's nothing really."

The marshal gave the young lawman a sidewise look. It seemed as if the people of Green River had a deep, dark mystery among them, and they would not share the secret with outsiders. Marksberry decided he could get it out of Sam Bodine; he would talk to him about it in private at the first opportunity.

Lamar Bodine was two steps ahead of the others when they reached his brother's house, turned into the yard, and saw the front door standing open. Stepping up onto the porch, Lamar stopped in his tracks, and the other men almost plowed into him. At the sight of the blood streaks smeared on the floor of the porch and on the threshold of the door, the other men also froze.

Lamar bolted inside, calling his oldest brother's name. The others followed, each man taking a different direction and checking the house thoroughly. After getting no response from Sam, they gathered in the back bedroom.

"The bed's made up," observed Earl. "Whatever happened came after he had been up awhile this morning."

"Or before he went to bed last night," offered Marksberry. "The blood on the porch has been there several hours—actually, I'd say since last night."

The four men agreed that everything appeared to be in order, and if there had been a scuffle, it must have taken place on the porch.

Leaving Lanny Hughes and Keith Marksberry for a few moments, the Bodine brothers separated and ran to the neighbors' houses nearby. Returning, they announced that the neighbors had heard nothing out of the ordinary.

"That leads me to believe that the blood came from a stab wound rather than from a gunshot," Marksberry concluded.

"Let's check to see if Sam's horse is at the livery," suggested Lamar.

Closing the door of the house, they hurried to the livery stable, where they found Sam's horse eating contentedly. The lawman definitely had not ridden off somewhere.

As they returned to the marshal's office they discussed the situation. Lanny Hughes said, "We need to get up a search party and comb the area. Sam has to be around here somewhere."

"Gentlemen," put in Marksberry, "it's not that I have no concern about Sam's whereabouts, but I really must be after the gang member who got away. Lanny, I need to turn my prisoner over to you. He'll have to be your responsibility until I return, or until Sam shows up. I think the doctor will want to keep him at the clinic for a while, so the best thing to do is handcuff him to his bed. As soon as I've tracked down the other gang member, I'll be back to take this one to Crescent Junction to stand trial for robbery and murder."

Frowning, Lanny said to the Bodines, "Since I've got to guard the wounded man and watch over the town in Sam's absence, you'll have to organize the search party for your brother."

Earl looked at his brother, and they both nodded.

"Good," Lanny said. "Let's get over to the clinic so I can cuff that man to his bed."

"I'll see who it is," Bertha Nash told Doc Guthrie and Bonnie Bodine at the sound of the knock on the door to the surgery, and she wheeled her chair across the room to the accompaniment of its characteristic squeaking. She opened the door to reveal the two Bodine brothers and two lawmen standing there.

"Can we come in?" asked Earl Bodine, holding his Stetson in his hands.

Doing a half spin with her chair, the huge woman said, "Dr. Guthrie, it's the Bodines with Lanny and a marshal. Is it all right if they come in here now?"

Guthrie was drying his hands near the washbasin. "Yes," he said, nodding.

Bertha backed her chair up to allow the four men to enter, and as Earl and Lamar stepped into the room, they seemed to bristle at the sight of their sister standing at the operating table, holding the hand of the stranger, who was slowly waking up from the anesthetic.

Smiling at her brothers, Bonnie looked past them, expecting to see Sam. When she saw Lanny Hughes, her face took on a worried expression, and she asked Earl, "Where's Sam?"

"We've got bad news, honey," Earl said glumly. "Sam hadn't shown up at the office when we got there, so we went over to his house. The front door was standing open, and there's blood in the doorway and on the porch. Sam's nowhere to be found."

Bonnie's face twisted in fear. "Oh, Earl, we've got to find him!"

"We will, Bonnie," he said, forcing into his voice a note of optimism that his face did not share. He then added, "Maybe you shouldn't be so friendly with this man. It might turn out that this stranger and his gang had something to do with Sam's disappearance."

Fully conscious but not yet fully alert, the wounded man tried to protest. "Mr. Bodine," he said drowsily, "I can't offer any proof that I'm not part of a gang . . . but I just know in my heart that I'm not an outlaw."

"I know you're not, too," Bonnie declared fiercely, still gripping his hand.

Keith Marksberry stepped up to the table and said, "Mister, I'm leaving you in the custody of Deputy Marshal Lanny Hughes. He's going to be responsible for you till I return."

"Speaking of which, Doc," Lanny said, turning to the physician, "can this guy be put in one of your beds now? I've got to shackle him so he can't escape."

Guthrie sighed and replied, "He really shouldn't be moved for a while, but if you fellas insist . . . Well, follow me."

Reluctantly Bonnie let go of the stranger's hand, her anger almost palpable as the two lawmen lifted him off the operating table and, as the physician instructed, carried him into an adjoining room that served as a small ward. Lanny Hughes then handcuffed the man's wrist to the metal bedframe in as comfortable a position as possible.

Laying a gentle hand on his sister's shoulder, Earl said, "Come on, Bonnie, we'll take you home. Lamar and I want to get back as fast as we can to start searching for Sam."

"I'll be going now, too," said Marksberry.

Holding herself stiffly, the small blonde stepped up

to Marksberry and demanded, "Marshal, how long do you figure it will take you to track down this other man and bring him in?"

"There's no way to tell," he answered, shrugging his shoulders. "It could take a few hours or many days. It depends on just how bad he's hurt, and how far he can ride till he tries to hole up."

"Well, let me ask you something."

"Yes, Miss Bodine?"

"How would you like to have a bullet wound in your side, another in your head, and be chained to your bed like a dangerous criminal, and all the while be completely innocent?"

"I wouldn't like it one bit," grunted Marksberry, "but I don't know that this man is innocent."

"Well, there's an easy way to find out. Bring those witnesses to the bank robbery here."

Marksberry seemed to chafe under Bonnie Bodine's steady glare. "That'd be highly irregular, miss. Besides, I've got an outlaw to catch."

"And you've got an innocent man to release!"

The tall lawman bristled. "I told you, I don't know that he's innocent."

"That's my point! You don't know that he's guilty, either! Look, Marshal, why don't you climb onto your horse, ride to Crescent Junction, and then bring those witnesses back here. Settle this man's innocence or guilt, and *then* go after your outlaw. As badly as he appeared to be bleeding, he probably hasn't gone very far."

Doc Guthrie looked over at Bertha Nash and saw that she, too, was fighting to keep from breaking into a laugh over this forceful little woman's having backed the towering lawman into the proverbial corner. Siding with Bonnie, Guthrie said, "Marshal, this man has a very severe concussion, and in my professional opinion I am convinced that he is not faking amnesia. I know a bit about this condition, and I can tell you that while it leaves the person who has it with little or no memory of his past, it does not change his personality nor his approach to life. In my estimation this man does not have criminal tendencies."

"We'll wait to see what the witnesses say," Marksberry said coolly.

"What you are going to find, Marshal," said Bonnie, "is that your fifth man got away, too."

"We examined the area in and around the cemetery quite thoroughly, young lady," Marksberry told her. "There was absolutely no sign of another man's leaving there."

"Have you thought of the possibility that the fifth man left the others *before* they got to Cemetery Hill?" asked Bonnie. "Maybe there were only four of them when they went into the cemetery, and this man somehow got involved in a shoot-out with them."

Everyone in the room could tell by the look on the marshal's face that he had not considered this angle. Without answering Bonnie's question, he cleared his throat and said stiffly, "Since I will grant you the possibility that this man could be innocent, I will see to it that someone goes to Crescent Junction immediately and returns with as many of the witnesses as can come. They should be here this evening. With this matter settled, I can then concentrate on finding the man—uh, or men—that got away." Excusing himself, the marshal made a hasty exit.

Bertha Nash exploded with laughter and said, "Miss Bonnie, darlin', you sure put his feet to the fire!"

As the others joined in the laughter the stranger spoke up and said, "I hope you haven't gone out on a limb for me only to have those witnesses cut it off, Miss Bodine."

Smiling sweetly at him, she replied, "I'm not worried about it."

"Come on, Bonnie," Earl said in an urgent voice. "We've spent enough time here. We need to get going.

Sam may be in danger or hurt real bad somewhere, and we've got to find him."

"Yes, you're right." Bonnie looked down at the man shackled to the bed and said, "I'll be back to see you soon. You just concentrate on getting well."

"Thanks for your confidence in me, and your help," he said, adding sincerely, "and I sure hope you'll find your brother alive and well."

Lanny Hughes gave Doc Guthrie the key to the handcuffs. "It's to be used only for emergency purposes, like if there's a fire or something." He followed the Bodines out the door, saying he would be back later. He was going to take Green River's undertaker with him to Cemetery Hill to pick up the bodies of the dead outlaws—and to look at Denzel Murdoch's grave.

"If there's anything I can do for you, mister," Bertha Nash said as she wheeled herself beside the stranger's bed, "just give a holler."

"Yes, ma'am, I will," he said with a grin. "Thank you."

The big woman spun the chair around and headed into the hall and back to her quarters.

When Bertha was gone, Guthrie pulled a chair up beside the bed and sat down. "Some gal, that Bertha," he said, appreciation evident in his voice. "She can do just about anything a person with two good legs can do."

"How long has she been with you?"

"It'll be seven months next week. It was really rather curious how she ended up here."

"Oh?"

"Yes. Bertha was traveling from Provo by stagecoach when she passed through here. She was on her way to St. Louis to live with her brother, an elderly bachelor. When the stage stopped here in Green River, she was not feeling well, and she came to me for some medicine. I told her she should rest for a few days before traveling on, so she wired her brother in St. Louis to let him know that she would be delayed. The next day a wire came back, telling her that her brother had died of heart failure. Bertha had no other family, and she had nowhere to go, so, feeling most distraught and upset, she came to me for advice."

The stranger lifted a finger and said, "Doctor, could I interrupt you just for a moment?"

"Sure. What is it?"

"When you speak of Provo and St. Louis, I remember them perfectly. I know exactly where they are and could put my finger right on them if I saw a map. Why is it then that I can't remember my own name, or where I'm from?"

Guthrie ran his fingers through his thick mop of silver hair. "That's a question that I can't answer, son— and neither could any other doctor, I suspect, even a specialist. Amnesia is a very odd thing. We just don't know why only certain parts of an amnesia victim's memory are wiped out. We only know that it works that way. I'm sorry. I wish I could be of more help to you."

Smiling philosophically, the handsome man said, "No fault of yours. Go ahead and tell me about Bertha."

Guthrie nodded. "Well, son, my wife had died a few months before Bertha showed up, and I needed someone to assist me and take care of the house. While talking with Bertha, I learned that she had been a medical assistant at a hospital in Tennessee during the Civil War. Well . . . since she had no place to go, and I needed the kind of help she could provide, I offered her a place to live and a job." The doctor smiled and shook his head. "Every day that woman surprises me with how well she works and gets around in that wheelchair."

"Do you know what's wrong with her legs?"

"She told me they're paralyzed as the result of a wagon accident when she was in her late twenties—it happened a few months before the war came to an end."

"How fortunate for both of you that everything worked out for the best."

Nothing more was said for a while. Then, seeing fear in the young man's eyes, Dr. Guthrie asked, "What is it, son?"

Worry creasing his brow, the stranger sighed and said, "What if I'm an outlaw, Doc? What if I *am* part of that gang? I'll either be hanged or sentenced to life in prison."

"No sense in trying to cross a bridge till you come to it, son," Guthrie said compassionately. "I meant what I told that marshal: You just don't have the mark of a bandit." Adjusting himself on the chair, he added, "In fact, you know what I'm thinking?"

"Tell me."

"I'm thinking that maybe you're a lawman, and you'd been trailing that gang for a while when you caught up with them at Cemetery Hill. They resisted arrest and went for their guns. Bonnie's theory of the fifth man's having left the gang somewhere before they got to the cemetery makes sense."

"Sounds good, Doc." The stranger smiled. "But I wasn't wearing a badge."

"Something could have happened to it."

The stranger's eyes showed the strain he was feeling. Glumly he replied, "It's possible, of course, but not probable. Let me ask you this. What are my chances of regaining my memory?"

"Well, son," Guthrie said, twisting his silver mustache, "there is no cure for amnesia. Your memory may come back a little at a time, or all at once—or never." He smiled and said, "I've read that some amnesia victims have had their memories return suddenly with a second jolt to the head—but I wouldn't recommend letting some crack shot zing another bullet along your scalp."

The stranger grinned, then became serious again. "So there's nothing I can do but wait it out."

"That's it."

The bell on the front door jangled, followed by footsteps and voices. "Excuse me, son, I've apparently got another customer for my services. I'll be back after I've tended to him."

When the door had closed and silence surrounded him, the young man felt a wave of despair surge through him. He was totally helpless. The only bright spot in this whole thing was having met beautiful Bonnie Bodine.

He felt a sheen of perspiration form on his brow, and he lifted his left hand to wipe it away. As he did so, he noticed a white mark on his ring finger, and there was a small callused ridge on its palm side. The finger had definitely worn a ring, he realized, and his heart quickened. Had it been a wedding ring? Had he taken the ring off, or might it have been taken by whoever had ridden away from the cemetery? That did not seem likely since none of his money was taken.

Perspiring more heavily, he began asking himself, *Am I married? Divorced? Widowed?*

His body tense and his nerves ready to snap, the confused and desperate man struggled to remember something from his past—*anything*—but it was like dipping a bucket into a dry well. He could recall nothing that had taken place before he woke up in the cemetery.

It was not until he let his thoughts return to Bonnie Bodine, picturing her comely face and remembering the touch of her hand, that he was able to relax and drop off to sleep.

Chapter Three

Deputy Lanny Hughes was deeply disturbed over the disappearance of Marshal Sam Bodine. The news about Denzel Murdoch's grave's being tampered with was picking at his mind as well, but uppermost in his thoughts was his concern over his boss. Until he returned to Sam's house to see if perhaps he had overlooked some clue to reveal the marshal's whereabouts, Lanny would not ride out to Cemetery Hill.

Hurrying through the streets of Green River, the deputy reached Sam Bodine's house and stepped onto the porch. As he opened the door and stepped inside, he was careful to step around the bloodstains on the porch and the threshold, which he then turned around to examine. Close scrutiny revealed that the stains had been slightly smeared by the soles of boots or shoes, probably those of someone leaving the scene.

Entering the house and again finding no indication that there had been any disturbance, Lanny concluded that when Sam Bodine had answered a knock at his door, his assailant had surprised him by instantly plunging a knife into his body. Since the blood was smeared only a little, Lanny decided that no struggle had taken place on the porch.

A shiver ran down the deputy's back. Since Sam had

apparently offered no resistance, the blade had probably been plunged into his heart, and he had no doubt died within a few seconds, his body pumping out blood for a short while after death. The killer must have picked up the body and carried it away, since there were no marks on the ground to indicate that Sam had been dragged. But who could the killer be? And where could he have taken the body?

Lanny Hughes knew one thing for sure: Unless there was more than one killer, the man who did it had to be plenty strong. Sam Bodine was a big man, weighing well over two hundred twenty-five pounds—and his dead weight would feel a lot heavier.

Shaking his head as if to throw off all these repugnant thoughts, the deputy tried to convince himself that Sam's assailant had merely hit him over the head and the blood was from a cut on his scalp. But even as the less-troubling thoughts filtered through his mind, Lanny Hughes knew there was too much blood on the porch to have come from a head wound.

Again a cold chill ran up his spine. Sam Bodine had been murdered, as sure as December follows November.

Feeling sick all over and hoping that somehow his deductions were wrong, the deputy made his way back to Green River's main street, walked to the Nugent Undertaking Parlor and Cabinet Shop, and entered the front door. Stepping into the office, Lanny could hear a tapping sound coming from the rear of the building. He parted the purple curtains that hung in the doorway at the back of the viewing room and moved past a stack of pine and mahogany coffins to where a short, middle-aged man—wire-thin and with a hawk nose and a protruding Adam's apple—was putting the finishing touches on a glass-doored cabinet. When the main line of business was slow, and there were no bodies to embalm and no burials to oversee, Arnold Nugent built cabinets to supplement his income.

The undertaker turned to acknowledge the presence

of the visitor, and his deep-set dark eyes probed the deputy's face as he said, "Hello, Lanny. Somethin' I can do for you?"

"You hear about the shoot-out at the cemetery, Arnold?" Lanny responded.

"Nope. Been back here workin' all mornin'. A cemetery seems like a funny place to have a gunfight, though. Anybody I know?"

"No. A gang of five men held up Crescent Junction's bank yesterday afternoon, then rode this way. Seems they got to fussing and started shooting each other up."

Laying aside his tools, the thin man said, "I guess there are some corpses for me to attend to."

"Three of them. The town will pay you the usual fee."

"What the town pays hardly makes it worth the trouble," complained Nugent. "Five dollars a corpse ain't much for all the diggin' it takes. I wish these dad-blamed drifters and gunfightin' outlaws would pick another town to die in. 'Course, if the town council would let me bury 'em in coffins, then I'd make a few dollars, but it's always the same story. They don't see any reason to bury a drifter or an outlaw in a box."

"Yeah, well . . ." Lanny responded uncomfortably, wanting to change the subject. "Look, Arnold, I want to ride out with you to Cemetery Hill."

"I can handle it all right, kid," the undertaker said with a grin. "I ain't that old yet."

"I didn't mean that," the deputy protested. "Let me start at the beginning. It was Earl, Lamar, and Bonnie Bodine who discovered the bodies out there. They also found one man alive—he's at Doc Guthrie's. But the Bodines told me something that puzzles me."

"What's that?" queried Nugent, putting on his hat.

"They said Denzel Murdoch's grave looks as though it's been dug up and filled in again."

Fear was suddenly written across Arnold Nugent's craggy features, and his eyes widened as his Adam's apple bobbed. "L-Lanny," he gulped, "you w-wouldn't be makin' a joke, would you? I wasn't on the jury, but when Denzel stood on the gallows and made his threat, he fixed his eyes on me for a long moment, knowing I was the one who'd be puttin' him in the ground."

"This isn't a joke—leastwise, not of my doing. I want to take a look for myself. Can we go now? I'll help you bury the three outlaws."

Arnold Nugent readily agreed to Lanny's company. Leaving his business establishment and locking it behind him, he led the deputy to the barn, where the thin man nervously harnessed his team of horses and hooked them up to his buckboard, quickly placing two shovels in the bed.

As the two men rode westward out of town, Lanny Hughes decided he should tell the undertaker about Sam Bodine's strange disappearance. Upon hearing the news, the undertaker exclaimed, "But that's terrible, Lanny!" He shook his head. "I sure do hope that the Bodine brothers will be able to find him alive—even though I can tell by the expression on your face that you doubt that'll happen."

Looking down at his hands, the deputy remained silent for the remainder of the trip.

After the wagon had pulled into the cemetery, Arnold Nugent eyed the three dead men, then looked over at Denzel Murdoch's grave. There was a faint catch of breath in his thin chest as he beheld the mound of newly turned dirt. He seemed almost to have to force his gaze away from the mound as he cleared his throat and said hoarsely, "We'll have to put the bodies in the wagon and drive them over to the pauper's side of the cemetery for burial."

"Okay. You're in charge."

When the bodies had been loaded into the wagon and taken to the proper site, Nugent and the deputy began the tiring work of digging a common grave for the three corpses. The two men were exhausted from their labors afterward; nevertheless the fresh mound of Denzel Murdoch's grave lured them like a siren's song, and wordlessly they walked to the site and stood beside it.

Arnold Nugent wrung his hands and said, "Lanny, you don't think it's really possible, do you?"

The deputy lifted his hat, wiped the sweat from his brow with his sleeve, and replied, "Only in novels about ghosts and vampires, Arnold."

"Well, somethin' weird is goin' on here. Aren't you the least bit scared? Denzel named you as well as Sam, Judge Granville, and the jury."

"Dead men don't come back, Arnold," Lanny Hughes remarked levelly. Dropping his hat onto his head, he let his mind drift back eleven months to the trial that had sent Murdoch—a huge, powerful, but slow-minded man in his early twenties—to the gallows for the murder of Nancy Yeager. The trial had been a quick one, and the jury had spent only ten minutes in deliberation before agreeing upon his guilt. When the judge sentenced Denzel Murdoch to hang, three men had been needed to subdue the prisoner as he raved and screamed that he was innocent. Standing on the gallows at sunrise the next day, the rope around his neck, Murdoch had again cried out his innocence. Just before he had taken the plunge to his death, he threatened to come back from the grave and exact his revenge on everyone involved in his arrest, conviction, and hanging—naming the marshal, deputy, judge, and jury.

Suddenly a horrid thought leaped into Lanny Hughes's mind, hitting him so hard that a gasp escaped his lips and his face drained of color.

Arnold Nugent looked at him and asked, "What's the matter? Are you sick?"

The deputy turned toward Nugent, his eyes unable to focus for a moment as the image of huge Denzel Murdoch standing on the platform of the gallows stayed fixed in his mind. He could still hear Murdoch bellow-

ing, "You'll be first, Marshal Bodine! Then I'm comin'
after the rest of you!" The condemned man was still
crying out his threat and naming his victims when the
trapdoor opened and his feet plunged through the hole,
breaking his neck.

Cold sweat beaded Lanny's face as he choked out,
"Arnold, do you remember what Denzel said he would
do to Sam when he came back from the grave?"

Nugent thought a moment, and then his face blanched.
"Y-yeah. He . . . he said he would get Sam first. He
said he would . . . climb out of his grave and . . . and
bury Sam in it!"

Even as his words came from his mouth Arnold
Nugent's eyes bulged, and he recoiled as though he had
been punched. Looking back at the fresh mound, he
gasped, "Oh, dear God in heaven, no! Lanny, you don't
think . . . it can't be!"

The eyes of the two men locked. "I hope I'm dead
wrong, Arnold, but I think I know where to find Sam."

The undertaker drew a shaky breath and swallowed
hard. "Lanny . . . Lanny, if Sam's dead and in this
grave, then Denzel *has* come back! And if he got Sam,
he'll get the judge, the jury, and you! Then he'll probably come after me because I buried him!"

Struggling to keep a grip on his own fear, Lanny
Hughes said, "Let's not panic, Arnold. Let's . . . let's
open this grave. Get the shovels, will you?"

While the undertaker ran to the wagon for the shovels, the deputy heaved a sigh, grasped the crosspiece of
the faded grave marker, and pulled it from the ground.
Tossing it aside, he mumbled, "Denzel, dead men don't
come back. If Sam's in this grave, I'll know I'm either
in a terrible nightmare or have lost my mind."

Breathing heavily, Arnold Nugent returned with the
shovels. Taking one of them, Lanny asked, "When you
buried Denzel, did you put him in a coffin?"

"Yes. Sam told me to, since we had learned that
Denzel really was innocent."

"Okay," Lanny sighed. "Let's dig."

The dirt in the grave was soft, and in less than half an hour the shovels struck the lid of Denzel Murdoch's pine coffin. Saying it would be easier to remove the lid with the coffin sitting on level ground, Nugent suggested using the ropes he always carried in the wagon. The horses could be used to haul the coffin out of the hole.

Minutes later, the coffin was sitting before the two men. The undertaker stared at it for a long moment, then went back to the wagon and got a hammer and screwdriver to pry off the lid. Handing the tools to the deputy, he said in a strained voice, "You'd better do it, Lanny. My hands are tremblin' too hard."

Green River's deputy marshal accepted the tools, and forcing himself, he knelt down beside the dirt-caked pine box. Brushing away the layer of dirt that clung to the lid, he could see shiny new nail heads appear along the perimeter, reflecting the sunlight.

"It's been opened and nailed back all right," he said to the undertaker without looking up.

"Yeah," Nugent responded weakly.

Lanny inserted the tip of the screwdriver along the edges of the coffin lid, tapping the handle with the hammer, and the nails squeaked in protest as he worked the lid loose. When he had it ready to lift, he handed the tools to the undertaker and stood up.

Looking at Nugent, whose eyes were transfixed on the coffin, he asked, "You ready?"

His eyes still on the lid, the undertaker nodded with little jerky movements of his head.

Taking a deep breath and letting it out slowly through his nose, Lanny Hughes leaned over and took hold of the lid warily, as if the pine box might be filled with rattlesnakes, and in one quick movement he ripped off the lid and let it fall. When he saw the contents of the box, he gasped, and a broken sob rattled in his throat.

The large body in the coffin was that of Marshal Sam

Bodine. The front of his shirt was blood-soaked from the multiple stab wounds in his chest. Even his badge was covered with the coagulated fluid.

Arnold Nugent's eyes bulged, and he whimpered as he pointed at the forehead of the corpse.

Carved in Sam's brow, the letters emblazoned in dried blood, were the initials D. M., and centered directly under them was the word INNOCENT.

Swearing loudly, his rigid face displaying both wrath and grief, the deputy's mind tried frantically to escape the truth of the situation. "Arnold, this has to be a nightmare!" he finally whispered. "Tell me this isn't happening!"

Chalk-white, the undertaker said through stiff lips, in a voice dead from fear, "It's no nightmare, Lanny. It's real. Denzel has done what he said he would do. He's come back from the dead to have his revenge. He'll kill the rest of you just like he did Sam—and probably me, too."

Rubbing a hand across his face, Lanny said, "It can't be. It just *can't* be! Dead men don't rise up out of their graves and kill people!"

"Account for it, then," challenged Nugent.

Lanny was silent for a moment. Then he admitted, "I can't. But there has to be some kind of rational explanation." The initial shock was beginning to wear off, and as his nerves began settling down he added, "We have to keep this from the population of Green River. There'd be mass hysteria if people thought Denzel was keeping his promise to return and kill everyone involved in his death. They'd— Uh, oh . . ."

Turning around to see what the deputy was staring at, the undertaker swore under his breath. Two local couples had pulled up in a wagon, apparently intrigued by seeing Lanny and Nugent standing by the open grave. Two men climbed down from the wagon and walked through the open cemetery gate, curiosity written on their faces.

From the side of his mouth, Nugent whispered, "What do we do now?"

Before Lanny could answer, the two men drew near, one of them saying, "Hey, Deputy, Mr. Nugent, we were just driving by and saw you standing by this grave. We heard about the shoot-out that took place here in the cemetery, and we were wondering if—"

"Oh, my God!" the other man exclaimed as both of them looked into the coffin and saw the face of Sam Bodine.

"Now, look, you two," blurted Lanny Hughes, "you're going to have to keep this quiet. If everybody in town—"

"Hey, you just dug Sam up, didn't you?" the first man said, his mouth opened wide in disbelief. Then he exclaimed, "I know whose grave that is! It's Denzel Murdoch's!" Clenching his fists, he wheeled and shouted to his wife, "Susan, Marshal Bodine's dead! They just dug him out of Denzel Murdoch's grave! It's happened, just like Denzel threatened!"

Both women wailed and grabbed each other as their husbands bolted for the wagon.

"Stop!" Lanny yelled after them, "Wait!" But in their panic they ignored him, and as they drove off at a gallop, the deputy could hear them shouting among themselves that the people of Green River needed to be warned that Denzel Murdoch had come back from the dead.

"What are we gonna do now, Lanny?" asked the undertaker.

"I could jump on one of those horses and try to stop them, but detaining them would be next to impossible. I guess it's too late now. It'll just have to run its course." He sighed heavily and said, "Come on, let's put the coffin in your wagon and get back to town. Take Sam's body to your place, and if anyone shows up asking questions, do what you can to keep them from panicking. But first drop me off at the livery so I can get my horse. I've got to ride out to the Box B and bear

the bad news about Sam to Thomas and his family. I'll
be back as soon as I can."

After leaving Lanny Hughes at the livery stable at
the far end of town, Arnold Nugent drove farther down
the main street and was met by a large crowd. There
was genuine fear on the faces of Green River's citizens,
and they forced the undertaker to stop the wagon so
they could view their marshal's body. When they saw
Denzel Murdoch's initials carved in Sam's forehead over
the word INNOCENT, their fear increased.

Though Nugent was as frightened as the rest of his
fellow townsfolk, he stood in his wagon and attempted
to calm them, but it was to no avail. The people were in
a state of panic and would not listen to him. The last
words he heard from the crowd as he drove to his
funeral parlor and wheeled the wagon into the alley
were that Deputy Lanny Hughes had better find some
way to protect them—and himself—from Denzel Murdoch's
ghost.

Hearing the commotion in the street outside his house,
Dr. Walter Guthrie stepped out on his porch to find
what it was all about. He was horrified to learn from a
passerby that Sam Bodine's body had been found by
Lanny Hughes and Arnold Nugent. That it had been
buried in Denzel Murdoch's grave made the killing
even more gruesome, especially since no sign of Denzel's
body had been found, but the elderly physician did not
believe for a moment what everyone else did: that the
hanged man's prophecy had come true.

The alarmed sounds of the gathering crowd filtered
through the walls of his clinic, and when the doctor
went to check on his patient, the wounded stranger
asked, "What's going on out there? Why does everyone
sound so panicky?"

"Oh, it's just some nonsense about Denzel Murdoch
and some silly prophecy he made. At least it *would* be
silly nonsense if it weren't for the fact that a murder's
been committed," Dr. Guthrie said angrily.

"Just who is this Denzel Murdoch? And who was murdered?"

Sighing heavily, the physician pulled up a chair next to the stranger's bed and said, "It happened almost a year ago. Denzel Murdoch had lived here in Green River for four years, since he was nineteen. I'm not sure anybody knew where Denzel was from; he just showed up one day and took a job at the feed and grain store. He was big and strong, but not quite normal in his mind—a bit slow in his thinking. Everyone in town liked Denzel 'cause even though he was a mountain of a man, he was very soft-spoken and gentle, and he was always doing things to help folks out. He had a heart as big as a barn and seldom lost his temper—which was fortunate, because when he did, he could be quite violent, but only with things. He'd rip a door off its hinges, break up furniture, that kind of stuff. He'd never hurt anyone. I figured the violence was probably just a part of his brain problem."

Shifting slightly on the chair, Dr. Guthrie continued, "About two years ago, Denzel took a fancy to Nancy Yeager, the eighteen-year-old daughter of the owner of Green River's general store. Everyone in town knew that Denzel tried to court Nancy, and while she felt no attraction for him, she did feel sorry for the young man and went out of her way to be kind to him. Well, poor Denzel mistook her kindness for love and followed her around like a lost puppy, and she didn't have the heart to turn him away. But Denzel was so sure Nancy was in love with him that he began threatening other would-be suitors with bodily harm if they came near her."

"How did her father take it?" the stranger inquired. "He couldn't have been too happy that more suitable beaux were repelled by Murdoch."

"You're absolutely right," Dr. Guthrie said with a nod. "And when Denzel came into the store one day, Henry Yeager finally told the young man to leave his daughter alone—and that's when things went bad. Denzel lost his temper and went into a rage, ripping feed sacks, overturning grain barrels—why, he literally tore the place apart. Just before he stormed out, he threatened that if he couldn't have Nancy, he'd make certain nobody else could, either."

"I take it the threat was carried out."

"Yep. Three days later Nancy was found strangled to death in her bedroom. When Sam Bodine questioned Denzel, he admitted visiting Nancy at her home when she was alone about the time of her death, but he swore she was alive when he left."

"What about the threat?"

"He insisted that he hadn't meant it, that he'd only said it because he was so angry. But that didn't help him in court. The jury needed only ten minutes to find him guilty, which is what everyone else in town thought, too. When Judge Granville sentenced him to hang the next day, Denzel went berserk, screaming that he was innocent. It took Sam and two others to hold him— actually Sam had to clout him with his gun barrel and knock him out. The next morning they had him in chains, and four men were needed to drag him from the jail to the gallows while he wept and begged for his life, swearing that he had not killed Nancy Yeager."

Pausing and rubbing his eyes, the physician then continued, "Denzel wept and cried out that he would never have hurt Nancy, repeating over and over that he loved her. But then, as the noose was placed around his neck, his whole demeanor changed. His face twisted into something frightening, and with a wild, animallike look in his eyes he vowed to come back from the grave and take revenge on the judge, the six jurors, and the marshal and the deputy who had arrested him. He kept screaming like a madman and repeating his threats till Sam pulled the lever and sent him to his Maker."

The stranger said, "That's a tragic story, but I presume justice was served."

"I only wish that were true," Dr. Guthrie said with a

sigh, shaking his silver-maned head. "At the very moment Sam Bodine pulled the lever and Denzel plunged to his death, three sons of a local rancher came riding furiously into town, hoping to stop the hanging. The whole town was shocked when they announced to Sam Bodine that it was actually their younger brother, Rodney Varner, who had murdered Nancy Yeager."

"So Denzel was innocent after all!" the stranger breathed.

"I'm afraid so. Rodney had told his brothers that he went to the Yeager house to see Nancy and arrived just in time to see Denzel Murdoch leave. He was afraid that Nancy had accepted Denzel as a suitor, and he grew extremely jealous and decided to press his own suit with her. Knocking at Nancy's door, he talked her into letting him in. Once inside he made advances toward her, and when she rebuffed him, he went into a blind rage and killed her. But his conscience ate at him, keeping him awake the night before the hanging, and when his brothers rose at dawn, he confessed to them. They rode as fast as they could for town, arriving those few seconds too late."

"What happened to the real murderer? Was he executed, too?"

"No. You see, his brothers didn't have it in them to take their own brother to the jail, so they'd left him at the ranch—not considering that he'd run off, which is exactly what he did as soon as they hightailed it into town. A manhunt was mounted, and Sam Bodine finally ran him down over in Colorado. But while he was awaiting trial, I guess his guilt became more than he could bear, and his mind snapped. He's living out the rest of his life in an asylum for the criminally insane."

"What a dreadful story!" the stranger exclaimed.

"It certainly is," Bertha Nash said, wheeling her chair through the door where she had been listening. "When I first heard it, why I was just horrified at so much tragedy. But I must say, it looks to me as though Denzel is doing what he said he'd do."

The stranger shook his head. "Surely you don't believe that a dead man could come alive again. You're an educated woman with a scientific background."

"That may be, but you don't know all the specifics. In Denzel's gallows threat, he said he'd come out of his grave and get Sam Bodine first, adding that he would bury the marshal in that very grave. Well, mister, the deputy and the undertaker found Mr. Bodine's body in Denzel's grave—and Denzel's body is gone."

"Yeah," Dr. Guthrie interjected, "and I'm afraid Lanny Hughes is probably marked to be next, since he helped arrest Denzel."

The stranger clenched his teeth, and looking back and forth between the doctor and the woman in the wheelchair, he said evenly, "Though Hughes may be next on the killer's list, I can flat guarantee you this much: It's not a ghost that murdered Sam Bodine."

Dr. Guthrie was about to agree with his patient's comment when he heard the door of the outer office open and, excusing himself, rose to leave the room. He was close to the door when it swung free and Deputy Lanny Hughes appeared, his arm around Thomas Bodine. Bonnie was behind them.

Thomas was obviously badly shaken. Lanny was partially supporting the older man, whose complexion was chalky. His daughter's face was pinched with worry, and her eyes were swollen from weeping.

Pausing, Lanny looked at the physician and said, "I guess you've heard about Sam."

"Yes, I have," he answered, nodding solemnly. "I'm so terribly sorry."

"I rode out to tell the Bodines about it, and the news hit Thomas pretty bad. I'm afraid it might've affected his heart."

Motioning the deputy toward the bed next to the one where the stranger lay, Dr. Guthrie said, "Let's put him over there."

"Is there anything I can get for Mr. Bodine?" Bertha Nash asked, her concern evident in her voice.

The physician named a certain sedative, and the big woman wheeled herself to the cabinet of medicines. While she prepared the potion, the doctor began to question the rancher about his symptoms. Doc Guthrie rose to take the pulse and blood pressure of his patient.

Bonnie stood and listened for a moment, then sat in the chair the physician had been sitting in, next to the stranger's bed. Putting her haggard face into her hands, she began to weep softly.

"I'm very sorry, Bonnie. I was so hoping your brother would be all right," the stranger said to her.

She lifted her face and looked over at him, tears misting her eyes. Her lower lip quivered as she said, "Oh, it's so awful! Murdering him was bad enough, but to mutilate him was demonic!"

"Mutilate?" the stranger asked.

Dr. Guthrie's head whipped around. Looking at Bonnie, he said, "What kind of mutilation? Nobody told us about that."

Bonnie's throat was constricted, and she could not speak. Finally Lanny Hughes told them, "Whoever killed Sam used a knife to carve Denzel Murdoch's initials in Sam's forehead over the word INNOCENT."

Guthrie, swearing under his breath, turned his attention back to his patient.

"It's happening, sure enough," Bertha Nash gasped as she wheeled her chair to where Thomas Bodine lay and handed him the sedative. "Somehow Denzel Murdoch has come back from the dead!"

"Bertha, I will not allow such folderol to be spoken in my clinic," the doctor said angrily. "It's bad enough that others are thinking such rubbish. I won't tolerate it from my nurse. Those folks out there are frightened enough, and if they think that we believe such things, this whole matter will get completely out of hand."

Bertha, her eyebrows raised and her thick lips pursed in indignation, shook her head slightly and wheeled herself back to the medicine cabinet.

"Well, since I guess I'm in charge now, and it's my job to calm them, I'd better do just that," Lanny Hughes said, turning toward the door. "I'll be back later."

Dr. Guthrie watched the deputy leave, and then he spoke softly to Thomas Bodine. "You just rest now, and you'll be all right. You've got to stay healthy for the rest of your fine family, after all. That reminds me," he said, turning back to Bonnie, "where are your other brothers?"

She looked down at her lap, a small sob escaping from her throat. Then she managed to whisper, "They're still out combing the hills for Sam. I . . . I left them a note at the house, telling them what has happened. I'm sure they'll be coming here as soon as they return home and find it."

Anxious voices came from the waiting room, and Bertha went to find out what the newcomers wanted. A few moments later she returned and said, "Dr. Guthrie, I'm afraid you're needed by an awful lot of worried folks looking for something to calm their nerves."

"All right, Bertha," he sighed. "I can understand why there would be so many nervous Nellies; I just wish they would realize there's nothing to be nervous about! Well, come on. They didn't come to see me for my logical and sound advice; they came for my medications." He put his hand on Bonnie's shoulder and said, "I'll be back as soon as I can. But don't worry about your father, child. He's had a terrible shock, but he's still a strong man."

"Th-thank you, Doc," she sniffed.

He cocked his head and looked at her intently. "How about you, my dear? Will you be all right?"

"I . . . I think so."

Giving her shoulder an affectionate squeeze, he walked quickly from the room, following Bertha Nash's squeaking wheelchair.

Rising from the chair, the young woman stepped over to her father's bed, taking his hand and holding it in both of hers. "Daddy," she said softly, "I know how much you loved Sam—we all did. And I wish there was some way I could comfort you. I guess it's during times like these that you miss Mother most." Her voice broke as she added, "I just want you to know that I love you and I need you."

Bonnie listened to Thomas's regular breathing and realized that he had fallen asleep. She felt relieved. Gently she laid his hand on the white cotton blanket and turned away. As she did, she felt the stranger's eyes on her, and she found herself blushing slightly.

Moving to a mirror over the washbasin, Bonnie eyed her reflection and shook her head. Pumping some water into the basin, she took a folded cloth and washed her tearstained face. Turning back toward the stranger, who had been watching her every move, she said, "I guess I look a sight."

"I think you look wonderful," the handsome man assured her, "but that's beside the point. You've just suffered a terrible loss, and losing someone you love is never an easy thing to bear."

Bonnie made her way to his bedside and sat down again in the straight-backed chair. "That sounds to me like the voice of experience. Have you lost someone close to you?"

The stranger blinked and replied, "I wish I knew. I guess maybe I have, since those words came out of me so naturally."

"Oh, I'm sorry," she said, putting a hand to her mouth. "I completely forgot about—"

"Hey," he cut in while reaching out to touch her arm with the hand not chained to the bed, "you're upset right now, little lady. Don't be apologizing to me."

The gentle touch of the man's hand was all it took. Grabbing hold of it, Bonnie broke down sobbing.

The stranger, knowing she needed to cry her heart out, said nothing. Instead, he squeezed her fingers gently, reassuringly.

When she regained control of her emotions, she let

go of his hand and wiped away her tears. "I'm sorry," she said. "I didn't mean to break down in front of you."

"Bonnie," he said tenderly, "it's all right. God gave us tears to use as a means of release. They're normal and natural."

Bonnie smiled wanly at him. Taking hold of his free hand again, she said softly, "Mr. No-name, how could anyone think you are an outlaw? No bandit is as kind and gentle as you are."

"I appreciate your confidence," he said, smiling in return, "but since I wear a tied-down holster, I'm probably either a gunslinger or a lawman."

"I'll vote for the latter."

"But I wasn't wearing a badge."

"I know, but there may have been some reason for that."

"I sure hope you're right."

Bonnie looked a long moment at the strong, rugged hand holding hers, then asked, "Have you been able to recall anything at all?"

Shaking his head, he said, "No. Well . . . not exactly."

The blonde's eyes widened. "You mean there *is* something?"

"I . . . I'm not sure. There's a name that keeps coming to my mind when someone speaks to me. I mean . . . like they should be using it to address me."

"And that is?"

"John."

"Just John? No last name?"

"No, just John."

Bonnie's smile broadened. "Well, since you're going to be around here at least for a few days, you need a name. And John it'll be."

Chapter Four

It was not until early evening that Frank, Earl, and Lamar Bodine arrived at Doc Guthrie's clinic, after having returned home from their search for their missing brother to find Bonnie's note. Hearing the raised voices of her brothers, Bonnie rose from where she sat, keeping vigil between the two sleeping patients, and darted for the door that separated the small ward from Dr. Guthrie's office.

The brothers turned at the sound of the opening door, and Frank held his arms open for his sister, embracing her tightly as she clung to him and wept anew over their oldest brother's murder. Fighting his own tears, Frank asked, "How's Pa doing? Doc says he'll be all right after a good rest, but what do you think, Bonnie? Will the shock of Sam's killing be too much for him?"

"He's doing much better," she assured them all. "The shock was great, but Doc's got him sedated, and he really is doing quite well. He's sleeping soundly right now, so I wouldn't go in to see him just yet."

Frank's face suddenly flushed and tears brimmed in his eyes. Touching her brother's cheek tenderly, Bonnie knew what he was thinking and said softly, "Frank, I'm sorry you didn't have the chance to patch things up with Sam."

His lips quivered as he responded, "I . . . hate myself for having been so stubborn. If only . . . if only I hadn't been so hardheaded, Sam would have been willing to bury the hatchet, but I insisted on keeping things all heated up and angry. And now . . . now it's too late."

"Sam loved you, Frank," Bonnie assured him, wrapping her arms around his strong back, "just as you loved him. Hold on to that. Keep the good memories and let the bad ones fade away." She held him, the two of them weeping softly, for several minutes. Then they released each other, and Bonnie moved to her two other brothers, hugging each of them in turn.

"What about you, baby sister?" queried Lamar. "How are you holding up?"

"It's hit me mighty hard," she admitted. "I had to hold up for Daddy's sake, but once he fell asleep from the sedative, I pretty well went to pieces." Gesturing toward the other room, she added, "John, the wounded man we found, was a real comfort to me. He's shown what a tender heart he has, and how understanding he is. I was sitting in there watching over Daddy and him."

Earl bristled. "Bonnie, I told you it might be better if you weren't so friendly with—" His eyes widened. "Did you say *John*?"

"Yes."

"Is that his name?"

"Maybe. It keeps coming to his mind, so I decided I would call him John."

"Nothing for sure, then?" quizzed Lamar.

"No, but it may be a start."

Earl spoke again. "Bonnie, this man may well have had a part in Sam's death. It isn't smart for you to get too close to him."

"He had absolutely nothing to do with killing Sam," Bonnie said crisply. "I'm as sure of that as I am that he's not a criminal. It's my duty as a Christian to show

him kindness, and my duty as a citizen to consider him
innocent until proven guilty."

"Big sister, consider what effect your actions and
feelings toward this stranger may have on Pa. It's bad
enough that his son's been murdered, but if it turns out
that John, as you call him, had something to do with
Sam's death, Pa's gonna be even more hurt if his daughter's been cozying up to the man responsible."

Facing Earl squarely, Bonnie said, "That won't happen. You'll see."

Angered by their sister's stubbornness, the Bodine
brothers threw their hands up in disgust. Lamar declared, "As long as Pa's still asleep, I think we should
go over to the undertaking parlor and view Sam's body.
I'd like to find Lanny and hear everything he knows
about the murder, and who he thinks might have done
it."

"Good idea," Frank agreed. "Bonnie, you be careful,
you hear?"

"I will, Frank. I promise."

She gave him a quick hug and a kiss on the cheek.
Smiling at her brothers with reassurance, she went
back into the ward.

Stepping outside into the cool night air, the Bodine
brothers were taken aback by the number of people
gathered in front of Dr. Guthrie's clinic. Lanny Hughes
was there, doing his best to keep the crowd under
control. By the light of the town's streetlamps, the
Bodine brothers could see a combination of fear and
anger on the faces of the ever-growing crowd.

"It's not Denzel!" the acting marshal blurted out,
about to lose his patience. "Some very mortal being or
beings murdered Sam, and I intend to bring whoever it
was to justice. You'll make it more difficult for me to do
so if you become a frenzied mob. Now, I want you all to
go home and lock your doors!"

"What good will that do, Lanny?" a male voice re-
torted. "Ghosts can walk right through doors and walls!
You're the marshal now. Do something!"

"We aren't dealing with ghosts here!" Lanny angrily shouted. "I'll admit I'm deeply puzzled, but I know there's a rational explanation for what's happened, and I intend to find out what it is. Now if you'll all go home and let me do my work, I'll be able to bring Sam's killer to justice that much sooner."

"You're probably next on the list, Lanny. Who's gonna protect us after *you've* been killed?" someone else demanded.

The young marshal clenched his teeth. The thought was not a new one for him, but he had been managing to avoid facing it. Taking a deep breath, he said, "That's exactly my point. If *I'm* not afraid of the ghost of Denzel Murdoch, there's no reason why any of you should be, either."

"Can you hang Denzel a second time, Lanny?" someone asked.

"For the last time, it's *not* Denzel Murdoch who killed Sam Bodine!"

Henry Yeager stepped up to the marshal and said loudly for all to hear, "Maybe he's right, folks. Maybe Sam was killed by the rest of that gang that shot it out on Cemetery Hill. Maybe they killed Sam, dug up Denzel's body, and put Sam's in its place. It could have been pure coincidence that made them choose that grave. If that's the case, then one of the killers is right here in Doc Guthrie's clinic. I say we put that murderer on trial immediately!"

"Yeah," another man added, "he was in on the murder and is faking amnesia to cover for himself."

Lanny Hughes's face was livid as he shouted, "I'm the law here now, Henry, and nobody's being put on trial until he's first arrested for a crime. So far, there's no evidence to warrant the man's arrest, and—"

"Then why'd the Crescent Junction marshal handcuff the stranger to his bed?"

The growing crowd broke into loud murmuring at Yeager's question.

Shouting to make himself heard, Lanny said, "Henry, you're real good at running a general store, but you don't know a thing about the law. It just so happens that Keith Marksberry has no proof either, just speculation. And as a matter of fact, he's returning here tonight with witnesses to the bank robbery, and they'll either clear or condemn the man. I'm not making a move until those witnesses have seen him—which is the only reason he's being held."

"But if they *do* recognize him, he'll be taken back to Crescent City for trial. Then what will we be able to do to him for Sam's murder?"

"If he was in on Sam's death, he'll stand trial for that, too. But as I understand it, the bank robbery and the killing that took place during it have priority."

A middle-aged woman shouted, "But that's not right! Sam was a lawman, and it's worse to kill a lawman than just a regular citizen!"

Other voices rose in agreement, and the crowd began to cry out for vengeance against the stranger in the clinic. Feeling the weight of the badge on his chest, Lanny Hughes was doing his best to keep the increasingly ugly mob under control, but he was starting to feel all too young and painfully inexperienced, and he wished that Sam Bodine were at his side.

Someone in the crowd spotted the Bodine brothers and yelled, "Frank, Earl, Lamar, what do you say? It was your brother who was killed; don't you want to see justice done?"

Lanny Hughes turned and looked behind him at the three men, and his eyes pleaded with them for help.

"Lanny's right," Earl told them. "What you're doing isn't going to solve anything. Lanny's the marshal now, and you've got to let him do his job."

Looking over the crowd, Frank Bodine declared loudly, "I'll tell you what Sam Bodine would say to all this. My brother would say you were making a mockery of all that he stood for. Sam would never have bent the law for anyone—least of all for himself."

Startled as much by Frank's words as his resemblance to his dead brother, the crowd quieted slightly. But after a few moments it became hostile again, and one man shouted, "Maybe Frank killed Sam! They had some bad blood between 'em!"

Frank's face flushed as Lanny Hughes bellowed, "That's a dirty thing to say, Jack Huggins! I don't want to hear any more of that kind of talk!"

Somebody else picked up a rock and threw it at one of the clinic's windows, shattering it. "I say that stranger was in on Sam's murder," the man yelled. "Maybe he was the one who actually stabbed him! Let's get him out here and ask him!"

Several of the men began to push their way toward the clinic door, and Lanny raced ahead of them, bracing his back against it. The Bodine brothers stood squarely beside him, forming a blockade.

"Get back!" Lanny snapped at the crowd. "Don't do anything stupid."

The sound of hooves approaching caught everyone's attention, and the young lawman sighed in apparent relief at the arrival of Marshal Keith Marksberry from Crescent Junction, leading three other riders and a surrey.

Assessing the situation immediately, Marksberry quickly dismounted and elbowed his way through the crowd until he reached Lanny's side.

Lanny Hughes told the marshal what was happening, and then, looking past Marksberry to the two women in the surrey, the young lawman said, "I assume those are your witnesses."

"Yes. The two women and also the man on the lead horse."

"If they identify our prisoner in there as one of the gang, we're in trouble. These people have already decided that if he's guilty of what happened at your bank, he's also guilty of killing Sam. If your witnesses do recognize him, and you try to take him back to Crescent Junction to stand trial, there's going to be bloodshed."

"Well," said Marksberry, "as Miss Bodine pointed out this morning, we've got a fifty percent chance that the man is innocent. Let me see if I can cool them down. Then I'll take my witnesses inside. If they identify him, we'll have to decide at that point what to do."

Many citizens of Green River knew Keith Marksberry, and when he lifted his hands and called out for silence, the crowd settled down and listened. Marksberry quickly explained that he had brought three witnesses with him who had seen all five of the robbers who held up their bank. If the witnesses cleared the stranger, the people must realize the man really was a victim of amnesia, and they had no reason to accuse him of having a hand in the death of Sam Bodine.

The people in the crowd looked at one another and nodded their assent, settling back to wait for the verdict of the witnesses—a middle-aged man, a portly elderly woman, and a thin young woman. These three people were ushered hurriedly through the office door, and then Lanny Hughes and the Bodine brothers stood in front of it and waited, their arms crossed and their feet spread apart, presenting a formidable front.

Although Dr. Guthrie had been inside his office, he had been able to hear everything that was said, and when Marksberry and the witnesses entered, the physician said to the marshal, "I'll go and tell my patient that the witnesses are ready to take a look at him. Come when I call you."

Bonnie, her father, and the man called John were staring at the door as the doctor entered the ward. Her face pinched with worry, Bonnie asked, "What's going on, Dr. Guthrie? Why has the crowd gotten quiet?"

"Marshal Marksberry has arrived from Crescent Junction," Guthrie said softly. "He has three people with him who were present at the bank robbery yesterday." Then, swinging his gaze to the man cuffed to the bed, he asked, "Are you ready, John?"

"Bring them in," the wounded man replied with a nod, his heart thudding against his ribs.

The elderly physician walked back to the door and called, "All right, Marshal, you may come in now."

Leading the three people to the prisoner's bed, Marksberry said to them, "Now take your time and look at his face carefully. Also consider his build and his height, even though he's lying down."

The stranger, his jaw tightening from tension, searched their faces for some reaction. From the corner of his eye he could see that Bonnie's face was drained of color, and her lips were pressed together into a thin line.

It took the three witnesses only seconds to look at the man on the bed, then at each other, and shake their heads. "He definitely wasn't one of the robbers, Marshal," the middle-aged man declared for all of them.

"I agree, Marshal," said the stout elderly woman. "I've never seen this man before."

"Nor I," agreed the thin young woman.

Sighing, the stranger felt his whole body relax.

Bonnie took hold of his unshackled hand and said tearfully, "I knew it. I just knew it! There's no way you could be an outlaw. There's far too much good in you."

Reaching into his vest pocket, Guthrie produced a tiny key. "Allow me to assist you in righting a wrong, Marshal."

Marksberry took the key from the physician and quickly removed the handcuffs, saying, "I'm sorry, stranger. You may not believe this, but I'm really glad to see you cleared."

"No hard feelings, Marshal," the stranger assured him, a huge grin replacing the look of fear he had worn moments earlier. "You were just doing your duty."

"And speaking of which, I'd better see that these folks are taken back to Crescent Junction so I can get a posse together again. We'll head south into the San Rafael Valley in search of the wounded robber, who no doubt has the bank's money." Looking over at Bonnie, he said, "I guess, Miss Bodine, that your assumption about the fifth man's having left the gang before they reached Cemetery Hill was correct. My apologies to you for discounting what you had to say earlier."

"I'm just glad you finally listened to reason, Marshal."

The witnesses filed out the door with Marksberry on their heels. Just before the lawman walked out of the room, he turned and said, "I sure hope you get your memory back, stranger."

The wounded man smiled and gave him a wave.

When the door closed, Bonnie gripped his hand hard and said, "Now you're free, John—free to do whatever you have to in order to learn your identity!"

"It's going to be a little while before he feels like leaving Green River, Bonnie," said Dr. Guthrie. "John's got some healing up to do."

Little points of light danced in the beautiful blonde's eyes as she gazed at the stranger and said, "I come into town often, John, so if you wouldn't mind my company, I'd be pleased to stop in and see you."

"I'll hold you to that offer," he assured her with a grin.

"I was just thinking," she went on, still gripping his hand, "you really need a last name. Since everybody's calling you *stranger*, why don't we give you that name? Until we learn who you really are, we'll just call you John Stranger."

"Makes sense to me," he replied warmly, looking intently at her face.

Guthrie walked over to the window and threw it open. "What say we let some fresh air in here—metaphorically and literally! We'll also get to hear what the good folks of Green River have to say about your innocence."

Out on the street, Marshal Keith Marksberry shepherded the witnesses back through the milling crowd. Then he rejoined Lanny on the top steps of the doctor's house and announced to the people that the stranger was definitely not one of the outlaw gang. His words seemed to reassure the mob, and the immediate threat of violence evaporated. But almost as soon as the witnesses rode away, Lanny found himself still faced with an irrational citizenry convinced that Denzel Murdoch had come back from the dead.

One man lifted his voice from the throng and said, "Lanny, this here stranger may not have been part of the gang, but we still have a dead marshal. Since the man inside had nothing to do with it, and since Denzel Murdoch's initials were carved into Sam's forehead, it seems like you've got to consider that somehow Denzel's gone and done what he swore he would do!"

"Wait a minute," another man countered. "Just because that man in the clinic isn't part of the gang doesn't mean that the gang didn't kill Sam—or for that matter, that the stranger didn't kill Sam on his own!"

"Neither of you is thinking clearly," Lanny Hughes shouted. "How could a stranger—or strangers, if a gang committed the murder—know enough about what happened to Denzel Murdoch to carve his initials in Sam's head?"

Suddenly a portly fifty-year-old woman pushed her way to the front of the crowd. Fanny Higgins was known by all to be something of a mystic, and while the young marshal was not eager to let her address the crowd, the spinster had as much right to do so as did any other citizen of Green River.

Fanny's double chins wobbled as she shook her head for emphasis and said loudly, "While you men are arguing about who killed Sam Bodine, maybe you had better consider something else. This town committed a terrible crime against humanity by putting an innocent man to death, and all along the higher powers have been extremely angry with us!"

"You're right, Fanny," called out an elderly woman. "We did do a terrible thing!"

Shaking a pudgy finger at the sea of faces, Fanny declared, "I'm here to give all of you a warning. Vengeance will be had for what we did when we hanged that innocent man—and I know by what instrument that vengeance will be achieved. Why do you think the man in Doc's clinic has no memory beyond his sudden appearance here? Why do you think he has no name? I'll tell you why. He only *looks* human, but he really came from out there!" Gesturing toward the starry sky, she said, "He is an angel of death who was sent here to exact vengeance for what we did to Denzel Murdoch!"

"That's ridiculous, Fanny," one man shouted, and many other people quickly agreed with him. But others voiced their accord with Fanny's theory, saying it made as much sense as anything else did.

Seeing that she had found some firm footing, the woman widened her eyes in an otherworldly manner and declared in an eerie voice, "Yes! Denzel is lurking somewhere in the dark shadows of this wicked town, declaring his innocence from beyond the grave as he did that day on the gallows, watching as the angel of death makes us pay for what we did. We must—"

Fanny's speech was interrupted by the appearance of the stranger at the opened clinic door. Every eye was riveted on him as, leaning on Bonnie Bodine's shoulder, he limped onto the porch. The stranger looked at Fanny Higgins and said so that all in the crowd could hear, "Ma'am, I couldn't stay in there and let this kind of reasoning go any further."

Startled, the heavyset woman blinked her eyes, ran her tongue over her lips, and waited for him to proceed.

In a calm and steady voice he declared, "Ladies and gentlemen, you must not allow yourselves to get caught up in some wild nightmare where spooks and goblins haunt the streets of Green River. People who become terrorized often do things on impulse that they later regret. Now, I mean no disrespect to this fine lady, but what she was saying about me simply isn't so."

Fanny Higgins glared coldly at the stranger.

Ignoring her, he opened his shirt, exposing the bandage on his side, and asked the crowd, "I ask you folks, if I were some kind of angel of death, would I bleed? Would I have needed the medical attention of Dr. Guthrie if I were some kind of ghost?"

Rumblings of agreement were heard from the townspeople.

"The man makes good sense to me," a middle-aged man shouted. "See there, Fanny, that hocus-pocus stuff of yours is just a bunch of nonsense!"

"That's right!" yelled another.

"Yeah," joined in a third man. "We're not dealin' with phantoms, Fanny; we're dealin' with flesh and blood!"

A frightened teenage girl stepped forth and said, "But, sir, if Denzel Murdoch is not walking among us, then where is his body?"

"The answer is obvious, miss," the handsome man replied gently. "The killer—or killers—deposited Denzel's remains elsewhere. This whole thing is meant to shock and frighten everyone. Does that make sense to you?"

The girl nodded and faded back into the crowd. Lifting his eyes, the stranger said, "Let me warn you, folks. Whoever killed your marshal—and it's apparently someone who knows about Denzel's threats and his innocence—may strike again."

Those standing close to Henry Yeager noticed that he lifted his hat and mopped away perspiration with a large bandanna.

Continuing, the stranger said, "If the killer strikes again, you must keep cool heads and not get caught up in hunting ghosts. That would only serve his evil purpose. Furthermore, if you get worked up into a frenzy, you'll start shooting at shadows and anything that moves, and in your blind fear you might end up shooting each other."

The people began talking and nodding among them-

selves, and soon the crowd dispersed. Stepping over to
the wounded man, the Bodine brothers all shook his
hand, apologizing for guessing wrong about his character.

"I told you he wasn't an outlaw," Bonnie said, smiling at her brothers.

"Yeah, I guess we should have listened to your woman's intuition," Frank declared. Then, sighing heavily,
he looked at Earl and Lamar and said, "Well, I guess
we should go see Sam's body now. Bonnie, we'll be
back for you and Pa shortly. Doc just told us he could
go home, and I think he'd feel better being with his
family."

Bonnie nodded. "I agree. I'll help John back to his
bed, and then I'll see to it that Daddy is ready to
leave."

As the Bodine brothers turned and left, Lanny Hughes
smiled at the wounded man and said, "I sure appreciate
your coming out here and giving me a hand with the
crowd, John."

"I was glad to do it."

"I've got a feeling that there must be a badge somewhere that belongs on your chest."

"Why do you say that?"

"You're an expert at handling a crowd. Seems to me
that you've done it before."

The stranger hunched his shoulders and sighed. "It
did sort of feel natural. I hope that before too long I'll
learn you're right."

Chapter Five

With his family in attendance Sam Bodine received a proper burial in his own plot in Cemetery Hill. Denzel Murdoch's empty grave was filled in, and though the people of Green River remained cautious, as the incidents receded in their minds, they began to fall back into their normal routines.

Two weeks passed, and during that time John Stranger was frequently visited by Bonnie Bodine, their attraction for each other growing constantly stronger. By the end of that time Stranger had healed sufficiently to walk slowly around town, and Bonnie occasionally accompanied him. Finally discharged from Dr. Guthrie's sick ward, Stranger took a room at the Utah Hotel and began sending telegrams to officials in towns and counties all over the West, asking if any of them was missing a marshal or was shy a sheriff. One by one the responses came in—each one negative.

After three weeks had passed, Green River was pretty much back to normal. Acting marshal Lanny Hughes had not come up with a single clue that would aid in tracking down the person or persons who had taken the life of Sam Bodine, but with the shock of the incident wearing off, all of the events in town were predictably mundane.

By this time John Stranger's wounds had healed completely. He could walk normally again, and his full strength had returned. He had even resumed wearing the Colt .45 and well-worn holster he had been wearing when he awoke at Cemetery Hill.

One morning he was taking a short walk around town when he saw Bonnie entering Henry Yeager's general store. Hurrying up the street, he dashed into the same building, loudly jangling the bells hanging on the back of the door.

Bonnie was standing at the counter, waiting while the shopkeeper filled her order, and she turned at the sound of the bells. She gave John Stranger a wide smile and said warmly, "I stopped by the hotel, but they told me you were out."

"Just taking my daily constitutional," he said, and grinned. "I'm glad I didn't miss seeing you."

"It was more than a casual call, actually. I want to extend an invitation from my family to have supper with us at our house."

Looking around to see where the shopkeeper was, Stranger lowered his voice to keep their conversation private and asked, "Does this mean that your father and brothers are willing to have me at their house even though they don't know who I really am? And that the invitation comes from all the Bodines, not just you?"

"Yes. They're all in agreement that you are a good, decent man, and Daddy wants to feed you at his table."

"You'll be doing the cooking?"

"Yes."

"Then I'm sure it'll be delicious."

Bonnie laughed and replied, "You'd better reserve judgment until you've actually eaten it. Daddy and my brothers certainly haven't complained—but then they're not exactly impartial judges, since it's either my cooking or theirs."

John laughed with her.

"How about tonight?" she asked.

"You bet. What time?"

Before she could answer, loud, angry voices erupted outside, one of which belonged to Marshal Lanny Hughes. Two or three men were shouting back. Excusing himself to Bonnie, Stranger dashed outside.

The young marshal, his face flushed with anger, was standing in the middle of the street facing three hard-bitten drifters, while one of Green River's citizens lay near the hitch rail with his head bleeding. The marshal was clearly angry.

"I told you to get on your horses and ride," Lanny shouted. "You had no cause to beat this man."

"He said somethin' I didn't like," bellowed one of the drifters.

"From what these witnesses say, you started the whole thing by insulting Fred," Lanny snapped.

The drifter peered around at the crowd of people looking on and growled, "They're liars."

Lanny's face grew darker. Pointing a stiff finger at the man standing twenty feet away from him, he said threateningly, "I'm not going to tell you again, mister. You three get on your horses and hightail it out of here—right now!"

The three drifters bristled, their faces hard and mean. "And just what if we don't obey you, tin star?" challenged the leader.

Lanny Hughes had learned from Sam Bodine to be tough and unrelenting with troublemakers, and he had faced this kind before. But always before, Sam had shown up to side with him and take charge; now Sam was dead, and Lanny had to act alone. Trying to keep fear from showing in his eyes, he swallowed hard and answered, "Then you'll get a taste of the Green River jail!"

Snorting with disdain, the drifter replied, "So you think you're man enough to put us there? I'd say you're a bit outnumbered."

Feeling his own rage rising, John Stranger stepped

off the sidewalk into the street and stood beside the marshal. "Maybe this will help the odds," Stranger said coldly to the drifter, fixing him with stony eyes. "Now there are *two* of us telling you to get out of town."

As a muffled silence settled over the street, the drifters looked at each other, as if to decide their next move. Then, facing Lanny and Stranger, the leader narrowed his eyes and blared, "We've decided to leave town—*after* we kill the two of you!" As he spoke, his hand plunged for his gun and his cohorts followed suit.

John Stranger's revolver seemed to leap from the holster of its own accord. He fired at the drifters before anyone on the street even saw his hand move, the loud reports echoing off the buildings along the street. Lanny Hughes cleared leather as two of the men buckled, and his bullet plowed into the third man a split second before another one from Stranger's gun found its mark.

Walking through the blue-white smoke that hung in the warm air, Stranger looked down at the three dead men. A bit stunned, Lanny Hughes said, "John, I surely do appreciate your stepping in to help me. They would have killed me for sure. There's no way I could have handled all three by myself."

Stranger shrugged his shoulders and stated, "I couldn't just stand by and let them gun you down."

As the townspeople crowded in to heap their praise on the stranger for coming to the aid of the young marshal, an impatient voice was heard among them: "Excuse me! May I get through, please?"

Stranger looked over to see a number of people being elbowed by a small blonde who was eager to reach the hero of the moment. When she broke through the press, Bonnie embraced him and without thinking blurted, "Oh, darling, I'm so glad you're all right!"

Overjoyed at her use of the endearment, Stranger was about to wrap his arms around her when Lanny Hughes clapped his shoulder and declared, "John, you handled that gun with more speed and precision than I have ever seen. Any man who can draw and fire like that has to be a lawman."

Stranger looked first at Lanny, then at Bonnie, and shook his head. "Not necessarily, Lanny. A gunfighter can do the same thing."

In the dim light of the dying day, John Stranger rode over a hill and onto the Box B Ranch and admired the beautiful spread. It was bisected diagonally by a noisy brook lined with willows and cottonwoods that wound its way through rolling grassy hills dotted with countless head of fat cattle.

The road, nearly half a mile long, led from the gate to the house, crossing over the winding brook by a sturdy bridge. As Stranger rode over the bridge, he could make out four men sitting on the broad porch, and when he trotted into the yard moments later, three of them stood and waited for him to dismount.

"Welcome to our home, John Stranger," Frank Bodine said. "Slip outta that saddle and come on in."

Frank, Earl, and Lamar greeted Stranger with handshakes as he stepped onto the porch.

"I apologize for not getting up," Thomas Bodine said, extending his hand from where he sat. "I'm still a bit weak."

"I understand, sir, and I assure you no apology is needed."

Just then Bonnie came racing through the door, her long blond hair flying about her shoulders. Admiring her ankle-length, rose-colored dress with its long sleeves, high neck, and nipped waist, Stranger felt his heart drum against his ribs.

Bonnie took both of his hands in hers and smiled warmly at him. "Welcome to the Box B, John. We are pleased to have you here. Supper will be ready in just a few minutes, so I'll leave you here for some man talk with Daddy and the boys. You like fried chicken, don't you?"

"Probably—although I don't really know."

Bonnie put a hand to her mouth. "Oh, I forgot!" She looked slightly embarrassed, and then she smiled and said, "Well, I guess you'll soon find out."

After Bonnie went back into the house, the men all stared into the gathering darkness and discussed the shoot-out that had taken place earlier in town. Lamar asked, "Did it help you to remember anything at all from your past?"

John shook his head and answered, "The only thing it did was raise more questions. Even my ability with a gun has done nothing but raise some suspicions that I might be a gunfighter."

When dinner was over and Bonnie had finished cleaning up, she removed her apron and announced to her family that since it was such a lovely moonlit evening, she wanted to take their guest for a walk along the brook.

Leaving the house with its windows shining yellow in the night, the young couple strolled alongside the babbling stream, which reflected the light of the pale moon lying low in the eastern sky. Unseen crickets were giving their nightly concert, and periodically a calf could be heard bawling for its mother.

As they walked, Bonnie told John brief stories of her childhood, speaking often of her departed mother and the precious memories she held of her.

Soon they passed over a gentle rise and were no longer in view of the house. Stranger paused, about to suggest that perhaps they should return to the others. Looking at Bonnie's face, framed by her long hair shimmering silver in the moonlight, he thought he had never seen a more beautiful woman.

Their eyes locked for a moment, and both of them sensed a quickening between them. Shivering slightly, Bonnie drew her shawl tighter around her shoulders.

"Are you cold?" he asked, his voice a bit husky.

"No, I'm fine," she replied in a half-whisper. Attempting to subdue the feelings suddenly coursing through her body, Bonnie made a half-turn and gestured toward a huge old willow by the stream's bank and said, "I've done a lot of dreaming while sitting under this tree and watching the water."

Her voice was soft and musical to John Stranger's ears, and he found himself wanting desperately to take her in his arms and kiss her. It was all he could do to restrain himself, and hardly able to think straight but realizing it was his turn to say something, he asked, "What kind of things do you dream about?"

Slowly turning toward him, she tilted her face and looked deep into his eyes, giving in to her feelings. "Do you mean before or after I met a certain stranger a few weeks ago?"

The implication was quite clear, and his heart burst into flame. Stammering slightly, he said, "Well . . . well, guess I would be interested in both. But especially—"

"Especially what?" she whispered, inching closer to him.

He found her so absolutely beautiful that he could hardly breathe. Licking his lips nervously, he uttered, "Bonnie . . . Bonnie, I—"

"Yes?" Her full, pink lips were alluring and irresistible.

"Bonnie," he groaned, "I don't know how to say this."

"Say what, John?"

"I . . . I've tried to fight my feelings, Bonnie, because it isn't right for me to mix you up in this complicated life of mine. I don't know who I am. I don't know where I belong. All I do know is I've fallen in love with you."

Their lips came together in a soft, tender kiss as he folded her into his arms and held her tight. She breathed warmly in his ear, "My darling John, I began falling in love with you the moment Earl and Lamar laid you in the back of our wagon. That's why I knew you couldn't be an outlaw."

Releasing her so he could look into her eyes, he drew a long, shuddery breath and said, "Dearest Bonnie, I want you to be a part of my life so desperately that it's almost the only thing I've thought about since we met. But I've fought it because of this." Raising his left hand, he tilted it toward the moonlight and said, "You probably can't make it out in the moonlight, but there's a white mark on the fourth finger—where a ring had been worn."

Bonnie took hold of his hand and brought it to her lips, kissing each of the fingers. "I saw that on the first day," she said shakily, her eyes misting, "and I'm aware that you may have worn a wedding ring. But, John, I can't help how I feel about you. I've fallen hopelessly in love with you."

He cupped her face tenderly in his hands. "I've fallen just as hopelessly, darling, and I'm completely torn by the way I feel. I keep trying to convince myself that it wasn't a wedding ring, that it was just any old ring. But the possibility that I may be married and have a family haunts me day and night."

Tears began to trickle down her lovely face. "I realize that if that's so, I'll have to give you up, for it certainly wouldn't be fair nor right for you to leave your wife and children for me. But . . . but until we find out, I will let my heart love you, and I'll relish the love you feel for me."

Shaking his head, he argued, "I can't ask you to accept a situation like that. I love you, and even if I get my memory back and find I have a wife, I will still love you. Since I agree that it would be wrong for me to leave her if she exists, maybe it'd be best if I ride out of your life right now, before we become even more deeply attached to each other."

"No, darling," she whispered through quivering lips, "even if I only have you for a little while, it will be worth it. I would rather have five minutes of your love than a lifetime of someone else's."

"But, Bonnie, it isn't right. It just—"

She silenced him by placing her fingertips to his mouth. "Don't say any more, my love. Just hold me."

They were locked together in each other's arms for several minutes, but finally they released each other and slowly walked back toward the big ranch house.

Once inside, John Stranger spent a short while with the entire family before etiquette dictated that he bid good-night to the Bodines. Accompanied by Bonnie, almost hating to leave her, he walked out to his horse.

They kissed again, and as she watched him settle into the saddle she said, "Let's keep in mind the possibility that you aren't married. Maybe the good Lord in heaven will let us have our lives together."

"Nothing could make me happier, Bonnie," he breathed, smiling down at her. "Good night."

"Good night, my love," she whispered.

He walked his mount until he was across the bridge, and then he halted the horse and looked back. Bonnie was still standing in front of the porch. He waved, and when she waved back, he put the horse to a canter, and the Bodine ranch was soon lost from view.

Riding through the night toward Green River, John Stranger was tortured by his blank memory, asking himself how it would be possible to fall in love with Bonnie Bodine if he had in his heart a genuine love for his wife—if he had one. He reasoned that if love is real in the heart, a blow to the brain cannot change it.

Then he shook his head. Audibly he said, "What am I trying to do? I can't draw any intelligent conclusions about this. I have amnesia, and I know nothing about amnesia. There's only one thing I can do, and that's to start traveling to every town west of the Missouri. I belong somewhere out there. Somewhere there's a town where people know me. I'll just have to ride and keep on riding until somebody recognizes me."

As Stranger rode past Cemetery Hill and the lights of Green River came into view, he made up his mind: He would leave Green River as soon as possible. Although the thought of leaving Bonnie was painful, he knew they could never have a life together until he found out who he was and where he belonged. He tried hard to cling to Bonnie's optimism that he was not married, and that they could have that life together.

Arriving at the outskirts of town, he could tell something was wrong. He heard loud voices, and the quick movements of lanterns and torches flitted through the streets like so many giant fireflies. Spurring his mount, he soon found that the citizens of Green River were in an uproar, and the focus of their attention was in the alley behind the jail.

Stranger wheeled his horse into the alley and hauled up, looking to see where their frightened faces were staring, and his breath caught in his throat. The gallows, built on skids and kept at the rear of the jailhouse, was occupied. Atop the platform was Marshal Lanny Hughes, shouting unheeded at the people to quiet down and listen to him. Hanging from the arm of the gallows, dangling beside the young marshal, was the body of businessman Lester Ames, his hands tied behind his back. The dead man's face was a bloated, ghastly blue, and his sightless eyes bulged from their sockets. Stranger knew that Les Ames had been foreman of the jury that had wrongly convicted Denzel Murdoch.

Quickly dismounting, John Stranger fought his way through the crowd until he was staring up at the dead man. What he saw made him shudder: The killer had carved on Ames's forehead what he had on Sam Bodine's—the letters D. M. over the word INNOCENT.

Lanny's harangue finally did some good, and the crowd quieted down slightly. But suddenly Laura Ames appeared with her teenage son and daughter, and at the sight of her disfigured, grotesque-looking husband dangling on the end of the rope, she let out a bloodcurdling scream and went into hysterics, and her reaction fired the crowd up again.

Her two children struggled with their mother, trying to get her away from the terrible scene, but she was out of her mind with shock and refused to leave. She kept trying to escape their grasps, attempting to climb the gallows to reach her husband's body.

Called upon to help by a townsman, Dr. Walter Guthrie reached the fringe of the crowd, pushing his way through. He began shouting to some of the men for help, asking them to grip Laura Ames's arms gently but firmly and bring her to his office. Three men quickly went to the aid of the teenagers, and soon Laura was being dragged away while she screamed her husband's name, declaring that Denzel Murdoch had killed him.

As he watched Laura Ames being led away, Stranger realized that the frenzied crowd was about to go out of control. Fanny Higgins was there, adding fuel to the already-stoked fire, declaring that Denzel Murdoch had clearly struck again, while Henry Yeager loudly accused Lanny Hughes of failing in his job for not having caught the killer by now.

Acting as if by instinct, Stranger dashed up the gallows steps, and when he reached the top of the platform, he yelled with all his might for silence. But he got nowhere. Abruptly he whipped out his revolver and fired three shots into the air, and finally the crowd came to attention.

When the roaring echoes of the gunshots had subsided, Stranger looked down at the people and said, "I warned you that the killer might strike again, and now he's done so. But you've got to keep cool heads. You must—"

Fanny Higgins cut in loudly, "You may not be an angel of death, John Stranger, but that doesn't mean it wasn't the ghost of Denzel Murdoch that's killed again. Look at Les's forehead!"

"Yeah!" came another voice. "Denzel's ghost is going to kill everybody who helped put him in the grave!"

Other voices shouted their agreement.

"Listen to me!" Stranger roared. "This horrible deed wasn't committed by a ghost! A departed spirit has no physical body, and yet it took someone with physical hands and great strength to knock Les Ames unconscious, then lift him up and place his head through the noose."

The people began muttering to each other, becoming calm and more reasonable as Stranger's rational argument began to sink in. Then Henry Yeager yelled out, "That's all well and good, mister, but that doesn't alter the truth—and the truth is that a killer is running around loose, and our young marshal has no notion as to his identity."

"Mr. Yeager, you're being totally unfair to Marshal Hughes. The only way any lawman can determine a killer's identity is by the clues that he leaves. The killer running loose in Green River is intelligent and cunning, and his only clues are the ones he leaves on purpose to put all you people in a panic, making at least some of you believe that Denzel Murdoch is carrying out his threat."

"Well, something better be done!" snapped Yeager, and he walked away.

Soon everyone followed the shopkeeper's lead, and with the crowd dispersing, John Stranger and Lanny Hughes helped Arnold Nugent take the corpse from the gallows and load it into Nugent's wagon. They were just finishing when an aging man, skinny as a rail, came running up, out of breath.

"Evening, Mr. Smith. What takes you away from your desk at the Utah Hotel?" Stranger asked.

Gasping, the clerk said, "There's been another murder!"

Lanny Hughes's head whipped around. "Who?"

"Judge Granville!"

"Was he due in town already?" Stranger asked the marshal.

"Yes. He always keeps his circuits right on schedule, and he was due to preside over a few trials tomorrow." Looking back at the elderly clerk, Lanny said, "Please, tell us what happened, Willie."

"Well, the judge checked in earlier this evening, and I put him in room seven—that's his usual room. He's been staying with us for years, so I know that he always wants a hot-water bottle when he retires for the night, and . . . and when I took it to his room a few minutes ago, there was no answer when I knocked on his door. I tried the door, and it was unlocked. I went in and—" Smith's hands went to his face.

"Go on, Willie," Stranger insisted.

Trembling, Smith told them, "He . . . he was sprawled across the bed faceup, and he'd been stabbed I don't know how many times in the chest. And . . . and Denzel Murdoch's initials were carved in his forehead over the word INNOCENT, just like—"

"Ooooh!" Arnold Nugent suddenly moaned, wringing his hands. Shaking like a leaf in the wind, he sobbed, "Lanny, you've got to do something! It's happening exactly like Denzel said it would!"

Lanny Hughes gripped the undertaker's arms and squeezed hard. "Arnold! Get a hold of yourself! Some cold-blooded killer is seeking vengeance for Denzel, not Denzel himself. You heard John. We're not fighting a ghost; we're fighting flesh and blood. It's not going to help for any of us to fall to pieces."

Stranger asked, "Willie, have you told anyone else about the judge?"

Looking up with fear-filled eyes, the little man nodded. "Y-yes. I met four or five men on my way over here. They saw that I was upset and asked me what was wrong. I . . . I told them about finding Judge Granville dead—murdered!"

"Did you tell them about the carving in his forehead?"

"Yes."

Stranger sighed and looked at Lanny. "There'll be more panic now."

Nodding grimly, the young lawman said, "We'll have to meet it as it comes. I don't know how, but I've got to catch this deranged maniac before he strikes again." Wiping a hand across his mouth, he said, "We'd better go get the judge's body, too."

Nugent dabbed at his sweaty face with a red bandanna. "Yeah. Okay."

"There probably won't be any clues, just like with Sam and Les, but I'd better check. Care to assist me, John?"

"Of course. You've got my help whenever you need it."

" 'Scuse me, Marshal," the desk clerk said, "but can I go now? I've got to get back to my guests."

Lanny nodded. "Sure, Willie. We'll be right along." He watched the little man dash out of the alleyway and toward the hotel.

Stranger and Lanny walked alongside Nugent's wagon as it drove slowly from the alley onto Main Street, and as they neared their destination they saw a group of men gathered around the front of Green River's gun shop. The door was open, the place was lit up, and every man seemed to be brandishing a new gun in each hand.

Lanny told Nugent to halt the wagon, and then he and Stranger strode over to the group. "Kind of late for the place to be open, isn't it?" queried the marshal.

Five pairs of frightened eyes looked back at him as one of the men answered, "John convinced us the killer isn't Denzel's ghost, Lanny, so we're going to arm ourselves and our families to the teeth."

"Yeah," said another, "especially since Judge Granville just got it."

Lanny Hughes realized that these five men—Utah Hotel owner Peter Condrey, hostler Seth Varney, saddlemaker Don Oliver, and shopkeepers T. E. Rockwell and Charles Mannis—were the five remaining jurors in the Denzel Murdoch trial.

Looking nervously around, Peter Condrey said, "It makes me sick that the judge got murdered in my hotel. I wonder if that's where the killer plans to get *me*."

"He'll get you wherever you are when he figures it's your time to die, Pete," Seth Varney intoned gravely. "He's going to get every one of us!"

Chapter Six

Earl Bodine was leaving the house and walking toward the barn when he caught sight of a horseman crossing the bridge over the brook. He watched as the rider, whom he recognized as John Stranger, trotted his horse toward the big ranch house. Waving, Earl waited for him to approach and greeted him with a smile as he reined in.

"Morning, John," he said cheerfully.

"Good morning, Earl. Is the rest of the family in the house?"

"Yes. They're all finishing up breakfast. If you haven't eaten, I'm sure Bonnie would be glad to fix you something."

"I'm afraid what's happened has ruined my appetite. We've had two more murders in town by the same maniac who killed your brother. I wanted to tell all of you about it—and then I need to have a talk with Bonnie."

Earl's eyebrows arched. "Were they the men who had been threatened by Denzel?"

"Yes. Let's go inside and I'll give you all the details."

They walked through the house to the kitchen, and Stranger greeted everyone, still seated around the table.

Bonnie's face lit up at the sight of the handsome man.

"Good morning!" she declared. "What a pleasant surprise." Then she noticed the grim look on his face and said, "Something terrible has happened, hasn't it? Oh, no! Not another murder!"

Nodding his head, he confirmed, "Two of them. One of the jurors and the presiding judge, who just happened to be in town."

"Oh, that's horrible!" Bonnie said, her hand going to her mouth. "Please, John, sit down."

"Thanks."

"Can I get you a cup of coffee and some breakfast?"

"Just coffee, thanks."

Making room for him, the other Bodine men began plying him with questions. While Bonnie poured him a cup of coffee, Stranger told them, "Judge Granville and Les Ames were both murdered last night, and the killer carved their foreheads with Denzel's initials and the word INNOCENT, just like on Sam."

The news struck the Bodines hard. Frank asked how the two men had been killed, and Stranger gave them the grisly details, telling them also of the crazed crowd and of the run on the gun shop.

"This is madness," Thomas Bodine declared. "Why, I know just about everybody in Green River, and there's not a soul among them who I'd ever suspect was guilty of such horrendous crimes."

"That may be, sir," Stranger said, shaking his head, "but somebody *is* killing off his fellow citizens, and I'm afraid unless he's found immediately, someone else will die. From what I understand, there are still five jurors and Lanny Hughes who were singled out by Denzel Murdoch for revenge."

"But surely you're not starting to believe that Murdoch's responsible?" Earl said.

"No, no. I just mean that whoever is doing the killing seems bent on carrying out Denzel's threat for him."

Lamar remarked, "Maybe the five jurors should leave town. I know it would be impossible for Lanny to go, but the others ought to get away from here."

"I don't think it would make any difference," said John. "Whoever is doing the killing no doubt would track each man down. I'd say the answer is for them to stay well armed and alert. After all, despite what some of Green River's more excitable citizenry may think, the killer is human—and that means he's bound to make a mistake sooner or later."

"But how many more have to die until he does?" Earl asked glumly.

"Only God knows that," replied Stranger, sighing. "I just hope it'll be over with soon." He looked pointedly at Bonnie and added, "And there's something else I hope will be settled soon—something I need to talk with you about."

Thomas Bodine rose from the table. "Well, we'll leave you two alone. The boys and I have to get to our chores. Be seeing you later, John, and thanks for coming by and telling us the latest."

"It's the least I could do, sir, what with Sam's death by the same hand."

Stranger and Bonnie were silent for a few minutes, waiting until the four men had left. When they had finally gone, Bonnie looked across the table and said, "I didn't sleep very well last night."

"Why not?" Stranger asked with concern.

"I was thinking about us."

"That's what I need to talk to you about, dear Bonnie," he said softly. "I thought about this whole situation while riding back to town last night, and I've decided that since my wound is completely healed and I'm whole again, I see no way to settle who I am and whether I'm married or not except by riding the West from state to state until somebody recognizes me. It's bound to happen somewhere, and then you and I will know about our future . . . whether we can have one together."

"I agree with what you're saying," Bonnie said with a sigh, "but it could take a long, long time."

"It could, but I just can't see any other alternative. I've got to find out who and what I am, Bonnie."

Her eyes brimming with tears, she looked at him lovingly and reached across the table for his hand, saying, "I understand, darling, and you're right. There is no other way you're going to find out. How soon will you be leaving?"

"Two or three days," he replied steadily. Pushing his chair back, he stood up. Bonnie rose as well, and he folded her into his arms. As she laid her head against his chest he said, "I'm really beginning to feel that if I'm not a lawman now, I was at one point."

Bonnie pulled her head back to look him in the eye. "Do you mean you've remembered something definite?"

"Not exactly, honey," he replied. "It's just that I seem to have some familiarity with the law and crime detection. Whenever I'm helping Lanny Hughes out, there's always a sense that I've done that sort of thing before."

"Oh, John, maybe these things are just the beginning. Maybe you'll soon be remembering details and even names. And once that happens—"

"Once that happens," he cut in, "I'll be back here to tell you who John Stranger really is, and I'm hoping with all that's in me that I'll be able to make you my wife." Then he drew away from her slightly to look at her face. "Tell me, if I'm not married but I *am* a lawman, will you still want me? As your husband, I mean?"

Looking up at him, she asked, "Why would that make a difference?"

"I was just thinking that since Sam was a lawman and he died wearing his badge, you might not want to be married to a man who wears one."

The beautiful blonde threw her arms around Stranger's neck and pulled his head down. Planting a warm kiss on his lips, she said, "I love you, John Stranger. If you're free to do so, I'll marry you no matter what you

are! I know you have to go, but I'll be waiting patiently
for you. And . . . and if it turns out that you belong to
another woman, I'll have to accept it."

Two days later John Stranger was packing his gear in
his room at the Utah Hotel, and although the thought
of leaving Bonnie for an undetermined amount of time
was tearing his heart out, there was no way around it.
Slinging his saddlebags over his shoulder, he left the
room and descended the stairs. He planned to say
farewell to Dr. Guthrie and Lanny Hughes, then ride
out to the Box B to kiss Bonnie good-bye and begin his
search.

Entering the lobby, Stranger stepped up to the desk,
where Willie Smith was in conversation with Peter
Condrey.

"Good morning, Mr. Condrey, Willie."

"Good morning," they chorused.

"I need to settle my bill," Stranger said to the hotel
owner. "I'm heading out to begin my quest."

Condrey smiled and replied congenially, "Your bill is
already settled, John."

Stranger looked at him curiously. "What do you
mean?"

"I mean there's no charge for your stay at the Utah
Hotel."

"Now, listen, Mr. Condrey," Stranger said, shaking
his head emphatically, "I refuse to be a charity case.
I've got money, and I—"

"Your money is no good in this hotel, John," butted
in Condrey. "You've done a lot for this town—like
keeping us all from going round the bend chasing
spooks—and I'm going to be insulted if you don't let me
do this for you."

John shook his head again and grinned. "When a man
puts it like that, I don't know how to argue with him."

"Don't argue," Condrey said, grinning in return. "Just
get out there and find out who you are. I'd appreciate it
if you'd let me know when you do find out."

"I sure will, sir." Stranger smiled. "Thank you for your generosity. And you take care of yourself."

Condrey patted his jacket pocket, which bulged with a revolver. "This should help on that score," he said firmly.

Stepping outside, Stranger walked over to the livery stable and saddled his horse, tying the saddlebags in place. Then he rode over to Walter Guthrie's office, thanking the physician and his assistant, Bertha Nash, who had taken such good care of him during his convalescence. Leaving there, he rode to the marshal's office, where Lanny again expressed his wish that Stranger would stay in Green River until the murderer was caught.

"Heck, John," Lanny told him, "it's like having Sam Bodine still around with you near."

"I wish I could stay, Lanny," Stranger assured him, "but that unknown part of my life is beckoning, and I have to answer the call."

"I understand. And I'd do exactly what you're doing," he said, and added with a smile, "but you can't fault a man for trying."

The two men shook hands, clapped each other on the shoulder, and then Stranger stepped into the street. He ducked under the hitch rail and untied his horse's reins, about to step into the stirrup, when a husky male voice stopped him.

"Howdy, John."

Stranger looked around to find the face that went with the unfamiliar voice. He found it in the person of a gaunt, leathery man in his early thirties whose deep-set black eyes burned out at him from under shaggy brows. Standing in the middle of the street, the man had the cut of a gunfighter, wearing a low-slung, tied-down holster.

Stepping closer, the gunfighter leered wickedly and said, "Fancy meetin' you here, John. Kinda out of your territory, ain't you?"

Stranger's heart leaped in his breast. Here stood a man who knew him—and he called him John! Quickly tying the horse back to the hitch rail, he walked toward the man and gasped, "You know me!"

"Know you?" The gunhawk laughed, throwing his head back. "Are you tryin' to be funny?" Backing away as he talked, putting distance between the two of them, he continued, "This day's been a long time comin'—but I told you in Abilene if I ever saw you again, I'd kill you!" As the bitter words were spewing from his mouth, his right hand was dipping toward his gun.

"No!" Stranger shouted. "I—"

But there was no time to stop the vengeful gunfighter. His own hand a blur as he drew and fired, Stranger managed to shoot the man squarely in the chest, and the gunhawk's weapon fired harmlessly in the dirt as he crumpled and fell.

Dashing over to the mortally wounded man, John knelt beside him and pleaded, "You've got to tell me my last name! I've got amnesia, and I don't know who I am! The Abilene you spoke of . . . was it Kansas or Texas?"

The dying man's eyes were growing glassy, and a sneer curled his upper lip as he choked out the words, "I'll get you when . . . when we meet . . . in hell . . . John." He coughed once. Then his body slackened, and he closed his eyes in death.

The people gathered around, congratulating Stranger on the tremendous speed of his draw. As he stood up, Lanny Hughes put his arm around his shoulder and said, "I heard it all, John. I'm real sorry you weren't able to learn your identity from him."

"No more than I am," Stranger growled, punching his fist into his palm.

The young marshal walked over to the dead man and studied his face. "Hey!" he declared, turning and staring at Stranger. "I know this dude. I've got a wanted poster on him at the office."

"What's his name?" asked Stranger.

Hughes scratched his ear. "Uh . . . Fletcher! That's it, Bruce Fletcher."

"Well, come on," Stranger said, hurrying over to Lanny and taking him by the elbow. "Let's go see if your poster has any other information on him."

Practically dragging the young marshal into his office, Stranger helped Lanny pour through a stack of wanted posters. It took them a few minutes before they pulled Fletcher's from the pile, and they read it eagerly. The poster did not reveal where the killer and bank robber was from originally, but it declared that his outlaw career had covered seven western states and territories: Kansas, Oklahoma, Texas, New Mexico, Arizona, Colorado, and Utah.

Rubbing his chin, John said, "I guess the best thing for me to do is to ride to Abilene, Kansas. If no one knows me there, I'll ride on to Abilene, Texas."

"We might be able to save you some riding if we wire the authorities in both Abilenes," suggested Lanny. "We can ask if Fletcher was even in their towns, and inquire again whether a lawman in their area is missing."

"Good idea!" Stranger exclaimed. "If it turns out that Fletcher was seen in only one of the Abilenes, I'll know where to start my search. That's good thinking, Lanny."

The young marshal grinned and said, "A man who wears a badge is supposed to be a clear thinker, isn't he?"

"Well, you're certainly doing all right, my boy!" Stranger said, patting him on the back. "Listen, I need to ride out to the Box B and let the Bodines know of this new development. Will you send the wires for me? I'll be back later this evening, but we probably won't get any answers until morning."

"Be glad to, John."

"Thanks. See you later."

As the sun began to set, Marshal Lanny Hughes was sitting at his desk, thinking about getting some dinner, when the scraping of shoes and boots directly outside the office door drew his attention. He looked up as the door opened, and the five town councilmen filed into the office, their faces grim and lined with worry.

"Come in and sit down, gentlemen," Lanny said, rising. "As I told you all when I asked for this meeting, I have an idea that might keep the killer from taking any more victims."

Two of the council members had served on Denzel Murdoch's jury. T. E. Rockwell, a tailor and owner of Green River's haberdashery store, had been in the midst of finishing up a large rush order, but he was glad to give the time to the council meeting if it meant saving his life. And Peter Condrey had willingly left his hotel in the hands of his clerk, Willie Smith, because he was eager to hear what the marshal had to say.

The other three council members were Sy Wheaton, the town's pharmacist; Clarence Roby, president of the Green River Bank; and blacksmith Jake Kidder, a huge man with shoulders resembling a bull's and muscular arms like tree trunks.

Lanny had already arranged five straight-backed chairs in a semicircle in front of his desk in anticipation of this meeting, and while the council members sat down, he struck a match and lit the kerosene lamps that hung in the center of the room. Easing back into his chair, he asked, "Do any of you have an objection to ignoring the standard rules of procedure and just letting me speak?"

It was big Jake Kidder who spoke up first, his deep gravelly voice resounding in the small room. "I'm sure whatever idea you have, Lanny, we're all eager to hear it."

"Well, gentlemen, the way I see it, we've got to fight fire with fire. There's a killer on the rampage in this town and we've got to take measures against him. I propose that we deputize a number of townsmen to patrol the streets day and night. My thought is to have two dozen men working in twelve-hour shifts, meaning twelve men would be on the streets at all times. I'm sure we'll have more men offer to do it than that, but too many men might make it more likely for somebody to get hurt."

Leaning back in his chair and lighting a cigar, Clarence Roby declared, "I think that's a sound idea, Lanny. And you're right, a dozen at a time would be enough. And this would continue until the fiend is caught?"

"Yes," the marshal said, nodding. "We don't have any choice. Perhaps with deputies patrolling the streets of Green River, our good citizens won't be so frightened."

"A thought just struck me," put in the banker, blowing a smoke ring. "No matter who is picked, we might be deputizing the killer himself without knowing it. Every man in the valley is a suspect at this point."

"I've already considered that possibility," replied Lanny. "We'll have to have the men patrol in pairs for safety's sake. And I think to ward off any suspicions against you council members, we should let the citizens themselves pick the deputies."

"Good idea," said Rockwell.

"I like the whole concept, Lanny," Condrey agreed. "Those of us who are targeted by the killer will surely be safer, including yourself."

Sy Wheaton interjected, "We'll need a town meeting, and it'll take time to spread the word. I doubt we can get everybody together before tomorrow evening."

"I hate to wait that long before putting the plan into action," said Lanny, "but you're right."

In full agreement to put the marshal's plan into effect, the council scheduled an official town meeting for seven o'clock the following evening. Each man would do his part to get the word to the people, starting that night. Calling an adjournment, the five councilmen left the marshal's office, fading into the night.

* * *

Marshal Lanny Hughes had a quick meal at the Sky-lark Café, then decided to return to his office and catch up on the paperwork that had accumulated because of the excitement in Green River. Realizing that he was a target himself, he thought it best to lock his door and draw the shades, knowing that a man sitting exposed by lamplight would be an easy mark for anyone with a firearm.

About half an hour had passed when a knock came at the door. Tensing, the marshal stood up, his hand going for the grip of his revolver. "Yes?" he called toward the door.

"Marshal, it's Darryl Cleaver," came the reply. "There's big trouble at the Wild Buffalo!"

Hughes knew Cleaver's voice. Relaxing his muscles, Lanny smiled to himself. The assistant bartender at the Wild Buffalo Saloon would certainly never be high on the list of suspects as Green River's killer.

Rounding the desk and opening the door, the marshal looked down at the little old man and asked, "What kind of trouble, Darryl?"

Excitedly Cleaver said, "Ernie Bain and Jess Gilbride were all keyed up like the rest of us over the murders in town, and they got more than a little drunk and into an argument. Only now it's worse than an argument, 'cause them fools each grabbed a whiskey bottle and broke it. Now they're threatenin' to cut each other up bad."

"Great! Just what the town needs!" Cursing under his breath, Lanny locked the office door and ran up the street to the Wild Buffalo.

As he charged through the swinging doors, he found the two men circling each other and swearing, each wielding his makeshift weapon. The other customers in the saloon were all looking on in silence except for Jake Kidder, who was attempting to talk the combatants into putting their bottles down.

But they were too drunk and too wrapped up in their

anger to pay any attention to Jake. Their faces flushed, Bain and Gilbride kept circling, each glaring at the other through bloodshot eyes and periodically swinging his bottle. The thrusts were punctuated with loud, profane insults.

"Hey, you two!" bellowed the marshal. "I want this nonsense stopped right now before somebody gets hurt! And if you don't stop immediately, I'm going to arrest you for disturbing the peace!"

But the two middle-aged men paid Lanny Hughes no more mind than they had Jake Kidder.

Stepping closer, Lanny repeated his order. But a jagged-edged bottle came within a couple of inches of the marshal's head, and he jumped back, anger showing in his face. "Ernie! Jess! Stop it right now, or so help me I'll lock the two of you up for a year!"

Jess Gilbride suddenly swung his bottle violently at his opponent. As it hissed past Ernie Bain's nose, Gilbride defended his action, shouting, "He accused me of bein' the killer, Lanny! When he apologizes, I'll lay this bottle down!"

"He's mean enough to be the killer, Lanny!" countered Bain while jabbing his bottle at Jess. "I ain't lettin' go of this bottle till he lets go of his!"

The young lawman pulled his gun and held it by the barrel, like a club. "I'm going to cave in both of your skulls right now if you don't cut it out!" he warned.

Ernie Bain saw the marshal's gun from the corner of his eye and paused, ready to obey. Jess Gilbride unexpectedly leaped in, ramming his bottle straight into Bain's face, causing all the onlookers to wince and gasp. The sharp edges of glass went in deep, horizontally slicing Bain's nose and left cheek and slashing through his upper lip.

His eyes bulging and his jaw slack, Bain's face was transfixed in horror, and a gurgling, raspy sound came from his throat.

"That's it, Jess! Put down the bottle! Now!" the marshal roared.

When Gilbride did not respond, Lanny's revolver came down hard on the man's head with a meaty, sodden sound, and he slumped to the floor.

Rushing to the victim's side, Lanny Hughes put an arm around Bain's shoulder as he stood wailing, his hands at his face as a crimson flow of blood seeped through his fingers. "Throw me a towel, quick!" Lanny commanded the bartender.

A damp towel sailed from behind the bar. Catching it, Lanny pressed it against Ernie Bain's face. With his free hand he pulled a key ring from his pocket and handed it to Jake Kidder.

"Carry Jess to my office and lock him in a cell," he told the blacksmith. "I'll get the keys from you later." To Bain he said, "Hold the towel tight against your face, Ernie. I'll get you over to Doc's office."

Several men offered to help, but the marshal told them he would handle it. Picking Bain up and cradling him in his arms as though he were a child, he shoved his way through the batwing doors and hurried to Doc Guthrie's house.

A few minutes later they reached the doctor's office, and while Ernie Bain moaned with pain, the marshal kicked Guthrie's door several times to get the physician's attention. Presently, lamplight showed in the office windows, and the door opened. When Guthrie saw the blood-soaked towel, he swung the door wide and said, "Bring him back here into the surgery. Who is it?"

"It's Ernie Bain," responded Lanny as he hurried through the front rooms and placed Bain on the examining table. "He and Jess Gilbride got into an argument and went at each other with broken whiskey bottles. Jess stuck his bottle in Ernie's face."

Speaking soothingly, Guthrie told Bain to let go of the towel so he could assess the damage. Peering at the wounds, he said to the marshal without looking up, "Get Bertha for me, will you, Lanny? This is bad. It's going to take a lot of stitching, and I'll need her help."

While Guthrie administered ether to his new patient, Lanny started for the door that led to the private quarters. Suddenly he paused, wheeled, and said, "Where do I find her, Doc?"

"Follow the hallway all the way to the end," Guthrie said. "Bertha's room is the last door on the right."

The marshal nodded and turned down the long hallway, stopping in front of the last door on the right. He knocked and waited. When there was no response, he knocked again, at the same time calling through the closed door, "Bertha, it's Lanny Hughes. We've got a man cut up real bad out here, and Doc needs your help."

The marshal waited patiently for about a minute, but all was quiet behind Bertha's door. He knocked again, repeating what he had said, but again there was no response. He started to turn away when he saw yellow light appear under the door.

"Hold on! I'll be with you in a moment!" came Bertha's muffled voice.

Finally the familiar squeak of the wheelchair sounded, then the lock rattled and the door came open. Bertha sat in her chair, rubbing her eyes. "Hello, Lanny. Sorry I was so long coming to the door. At my age it takes longer to get functional. What's the problem?"

"I'll explain it as we go," he said. "Doc needs you immediately."

Pushing the wheelchair down the long hallway, Lanny quickly told her what had happened to Ernie Bain. They entered the room to find that Guthrie had already laid out his instruments and was ready to begin surgery. Looking at Bertha over his glasses, the doctor said with a crooked grin, "I was about to start without you. You must've been having quite a dream."

Bertha's face flushed slightly, and then she displayed her usual professional demeanor.

Lanny Hughes stood by for over an hour as the doctor and his assistant labored to patch up Bain's face.

When the job was finished, the young lawman asked, "What do you think, Doc? Will Ernie ever look normal again?"

Guthrie glanced down at his sleeping patient and replied, "His face is quite swollen now, but he won't look so bad when the swelling goes down. I'm afraid he's going to be scarred pretty badly, though. Especially his nose. I pulled it together as best as I could, but the cartilage was severed. He's going to look like some wild beast took a bite out of it."

Lanny shook his head sadly. "Too bad. Well, I guess I've got to fine Jess Gilbride for this. He ought to at least pay your bill. How much will it be?"

"Call it an even fifteen dollars."

Lanny nodded and headed for the door. "I'll be around with the money tomorrow. Right now I've got to make my rounds and put Green River to bed. Good night."

Walking out into the street, Lanny followed his usual pattern, checking doors along one side of the dimly lit street, and then crossing over and starting down the other side. When he came to T. E. Rockwell's clothing store, he noted that a lamp was burning brightly inside. He tried the doorknob, but it was locked. A tap on the door window brought Rockwell from his workbench in the back of the shop to the front room.

A shade was drawn over the glass, and the tailor pulled it aside slightly. Seeing who it was, he opened the door.

"Hello, Lanny," the tailor said with a smile. "Making your rounds?"

"Uh-huh. Working late, aren't you?"

"Yes. Business has been almost too good lately. I've got several suits to make, and I'm way behind schedule. No choice but to work nights getting caught up."

"I'm glad you're keeping your door locked. Do you have a weapon with you?"

"Yes, sir! I've got a brand new Remington .44 repeater rifle. Keep it right beside me at my worktable."

"Good," Lanny said, reassured. "Do you carry it with you between here and your house?"

"Wouldn't be without it."

"Okay. Well, I'll be on my way. See you tomorrow."

"You bet," replied Rockwell. "I'll feel better once we have those deputies walking the streets."

"Me, too," agreed Lanny. "Good night."

Lanny waited until he heard Rockwell lock his door, and then he walked on. Moving down the street, he found all the other shops and stores in the business district dark and closed up tight. He was about to head for home when he saw a dark figure in the shadows ahead of him. Squinting at the large, bulky shape, he figured it was Jake Kidder, looking for him to return his keys.

"Jake, is that you? Thanks for bringing the keys back, but it wasn't necessary."

The figure moved closer to him.

Lanny's eyes opened wide. "Oh, Good Lord! How is it possible—"

A blunt instrument hissed through the darkness, striking the marshal hard on the head, and Lanny Hughes went down in a crumpled heap. Then he was picked up, hoisted onto an enormous shoulder, and carried away into the night.

Chapter Seven

The sun filtered through John Stranger's hotel room window, waking him. Opening his eyes, he could tell by the light what time it was and was surprised at having slept so late, since he normally awoke at the crack of dawn. Climbing out of bed, he crossed the room and turned the faucet in the washbasin, pleased with this modern convenience, and then he lathered his face and unfolded his razor, wetting it.

While he shaved, he recalled how excited Bonnie Bodine had been the night before when she learned of the new development. Although Bruce Fletcher had not supplied Stranger with his real last name or which Abilene he had referred to, the amnesia victim now had something concrete to go on. At least he would not have to wander all over the West hoping someone somewhere would eventually recognize him. Even if he had to go to both Abilenes, his search had been narrowed down considerably. Should it turn out that neither Abilene was his hometown, surely somebody in whichever one it was where he and Fletcher had last had a run-in would know him.

Stranger pictured Bonnie's lovely face in the moonlight as he had last seen her the night before, and he could still taste the sweetness of her warm kisses on his lips. Marveling at what a wonderful woman she was and at his good fortune that she had fallen in love with him, he wished that there were no complications in his life . . . that they could just get married and live happily ever after, as in the storybooks. He hated their joy's being marred by the uncertainty of their future.

Loving Bonnie even more because of her unselfish willingness to give him up if he was already married, Stranger laid down his straight razor, washed the remaining soap from his face, and said aloud, "Bonnie darling, you deserve a whole lot better situation than this one." He sighed, shook his head, and then hurriedly finished his grooming.

After he had dressed, he left the hotel, going to one of Green River's cafés for breakfast. Then, wanting to be at the telegraph office when it opened, he sauntered down the street at three minutes before eight, feeling certain that the replies to Lanny Hughes's wires would come through early.

When he entered the telegraph office, the second reply was just in the process of coming in. The telegraph operator handed both messages to him, and Stranger was surprised to learn that Bruce Fletcher had been seen in both Abilenes within the past several months and had killed men in shoot-outs in both towns. Again, neither town reported a lawman missing.

Stepping back outside on the boardwalk, Stranger was momentarily at a loss. He had been so hopeful that a telegraphed reply would eliminate the need to journey to one of the Abilenes. Now he was again faced with having to visit both. Weighing the options, he decided that he would ride to Abilene, Kansas, first, since it was closer. If he was not known there, he would then continue on to Abilene, Texas.

He headed down the street toward the marshal's office, wanting to tell Lanny Hughes his plans. Afterward he intended to ride to the Box B and say good-bye to Bonnie for the final time.

Reaching the marshal's office, he stepped inside and found it empty. He walked into the cell area at the rear of the jail, calling Lanny's name.

"Where's Hughes?" an angry voice suddenly demanded.

Stranger walked up to the prisoner's cell, staring at the angry face glaring at him through the bars. "I don't know," he answered. "I'm wanting to see him myself." Tilting his head slightly, he asked, "What are you in here for? I know your face, but I've never heard your name."

"My name's Jess Gilbride," the prisoner snapped, "and I'm in here for pushin' a broken whiskey bottle into Ernie Bain's puss. I'm sorry I done it, but I was drunk and—well, you know how it is. But it ain't right for a man to be locked up and then just forgot. The marshal's supposed to see that I'm fed. It's the law!"

"You haven't seen him this morning?"

"Nope, and I figure it's past nine o'clock. A man could starve to death!"

"It's actually just a bit past eight-thirty," John advised him, "but something *is* wrong here. You didn't hear Lanny in the office earlier?"

"Nope. Nobody's been in the office since Jake Kidder brought me in here last night and locked me up."

"Jake Kidder? Why did he lock you up?"

"Because Lanny was takin' Ernie to Doc Guthrie's to get sewed up. Leastways, that's what Jake told me when I come to as he was puttin' me on the cot here in the cell."

Knowing that Lanny Hughes was on Denzel Murdoch's list, John Stranger felt a cold knot in his stomach. He wheeled and dashed from the jail, with Jess Gilbride shouting after him to bring him something to eat.

Rushing from the office, he went in search of the young lawman. He asked several passersby if they had seen Lanny, but none of them had. Then he saw Peter Condrey standing on the porch of his hotel and went up to him, asking, "Mr. Condrey, have you seen Lanny this morning?"

"Not yet. He's not in his office?"

"No. He hasn't yet been there this morning, according to Jess Gilbride, who's locked in a cell."

"Let's go to his house," suggested Condrey. "It's only a few blocks away."

The two men hurried to Lanny Hughes's small house but found it empty, as well. Going back to the main street, they came upon the other council members, who were spreading the word about the upcoming meeting that evening. Stranger and the hotel owner inquired if any of them had seen the marshal.

"I haven't seen him," Sy Wheaton said, shaking his head. "Do you figure something's happened to him, John?"

"I'm not sure. I'll keep you posted."

A quick check at the stable revealed that Lanny's horse was there. This settled any question that he had ridden out of town for some reason.

"There's Clarence Roby in front of the bank," Condrey said, pointing across the street. "Let's go ask him."

Crossing over, the two men repeated their question, but Roby had not seen Lanny either.

All three of them then hurried to T. E. Rockwell's haberdashery. The tailor told them, "Lanny stopped by my shop when he was doing his rounds last night, but that was the last time I saw him. Let's see whether Jake's had contact with him."

As they headed up the street to Jake Kidder's blacksmith shop, Stranger was deeply concerned. So far he had found no one in Green River who had laid eyes on Lanny Hughes that morning.

Reaching the blacksmith's, Stranger told the burly man, "I talked to Jess Gilbride in the jail. He said you carried him there last night and locked him up because Lanny was taking Ernie Bain to Doc's office."

"Right." Jake nodded.

"Then Doc might have been the last one to see Lanny last night."

"I don't think so," spoke up Rockwell. "When I saw Lanny, it was real late. He didn't say anything about the fight between Ernie and Jess, but the saloons were closed by that time. So I'd guess I saw him after Doc did."

"He may have gone back to the clinic," suggested Jake. "Let's check with Doc."

"I'll do that, Jake," said Stranger. "Do you still have Lanny's keys?"

"Nope. After I locked Jess in the cell, I figured Lanny'd be back to look in on Jess after he did his rounds, so I put the keys in the desk and left the front door unlocked."

"You ought to see that Jess gets fed," Stranger suggested.

"Probably we oughta just let him out," said Jake. "I don't think Lanny will want to hold him. Ernie was wielding a bottle, too, so if Jess is sobered up, I think we oughta let him go."

"Lanny will no doubt make Jess pay Ernie's doctor bill," Roby offered, "but Jess isn't going anywhere, so Lanny can get it from him later."

T. E. Rockwell said, "Look at it this way, fellas: If we let him out, he can feed himself, and we won't have to worry about him."

The councilmen agreed, and Jake Kidder headed up the street to release Jess Gilbride from the jail.

Stranger told the others that he would talk to Doc Guthrie and see if he might have any idea as to Lanny's whereabouts, and then he would contact the councilmen and let them know if he had learned anything.

Standing on the front steps of the doctor's large house after speaking with Guthrie and Bertha, Stranger felt fear scratching at his mind. Apparently the last person to see Lanny Hughes the previous night was T. E.

Rockwell, meaning if something had happened to the young marshal, it had to have happened while he was finishing his rounds or while he was walking home.

A thought that hit him like icy water sprang into Stranger's mind. Hoping he was wrong, he dashed to the stable, saddled his horse, and headed west out of town.

Guiding his horse off the road into Cemetery Hill, he skidded to a halt by the gate and ran into the graveyard. He stopped short a few yards from what had been Denzel Murdoch's grave.

Stranger knew that after Sam Bodine had been reburied in his own plot, Arnold Nugent had filled in Denzel's grave, tamping it flat and discarding the marker. A sick horror came over Stranger when he saw a fresh mound where first Denzel, then Sam had been buried, and at its head stood a crude wooden marker.

Walking slowly toward the freshly turned soil, his legs feeling like lead, Stranger knew what the marker would say even before he was close enough to read it. Scratched crudely on its rough surface were the words:

Here Lies Lanny Hughes
He Helped Arrest Me
I Was Innocent
D. M.

"Dear God, no," he choked out, feeling numb all over. "Not Lanny. He was still a kid."

He turned and, shoulders slumped, headed over to his horse, riding hurriedly back into town.

After Stranger had alerted the council members to his discovery, they quickly rounded up Walter Guthrie and Arnold Nugent. With the elderly physician riding in Nugent's wagon, the procession returned to the cemetery.

A breeze blew across the graveyard as the eight men

stood over the fresh mound. Eyeing the grave marker, Peter Condrey swore, then said, "Who's doing this terrible thing to us? I want this to be just some horrible nightmare that I'll wake up from at any moment."

"If we knew who it was, the nightmare would be over for all of us," said Jake Kidder. "We'd *make* him stop."

"If we *could* stop him," T. E. Rockwell said nervously.

Jake screwed up his beefy face and asked, "What do you mean by that?"

"I mean, maybe it is Denzel! That's what I mean!" Rockwell practically screamed.

"You're letting this get in the way of logic," Clarence Roby said. "It's not Denzel. John and Lanny both pointed out quite clearly to all of us that this ghost stuff is ridiculous."

Rockwell, his face white as a sheet, did not reply.

Arnold Nugent, who was jittery himself, pulled three shovels from the wagon, handing two of them to those who reached for them first. In less than an hour they exhumed the body of Lanny Hughes, laying it gently on the ground. Kneeling beside the body, wiping away the moist dirt that clung to the clothing and skin, Doc Guthrie uncovered the same mutilating carving on the forehead as the other victims had had. Then the physician did a thorough examination.

When he was finished, Guthrie stood up, sighed, and said to the group, "Whoever did this is a very powerful man. Lanny's neck is broken. He was hit on the head first—quite hard, in fact—but it wasn't the blow on the head that killed him. He died when the murderer snapped his neck." He shuddered slightly and added, "I only hope poor Lanny never regained consciousness so he never knew he was going to die."

John Stranger studied the body, then knelt and pulled Lanny's dirt-caked revolver from its holster. Breaking it open, he saw that it was fully loaded, and that none of the bullets had been fired. "This suggests that Lanny knew his assailant," he mused aloud.

The others all looked at him, clearly wondering why he would make that assumption.

Proceeding, he said, "His gun was still in the holster, which means that either he didn't think the man he saw was the killer or he was so surprised by the killer that he didn't have time to react. Otherwise he would've drawn the gun and fired it. And by the location of the bruise on his head, it's evident that Lanny was facing the man who hit him, and the killer had to have been very close to him."

"Makes sense," said Peter Condrey, nodding.

Rockwell was trembling. "M-maybe not," he said shakily. "Maybe he drew his gun, but didn't get a chance to fire it. Maybe the killer put it back in the holster after Lanny went down under the blow."

"I doubt it," countered Stranger. "I don't think the killer would have taken the time to bother with the gun if it had fallen to the ground."

"I think you're wrong," said Rockwell. "I think the person who killed Lanny was Denzel Murdoch! You heard what Doc said. The man who broke Lanny's neck was very strong—and Denzel Murdoch was as strong as an elephant!"

Stranger again tried to squelch the ghost idea, but he could see uncertainty in the eyes of some of the men. The undertaker seemed especially vulnerable to this irrational conclusion, and Stranger worried that once Fanny Higgins got word of Lanny's death, she would incite others like Nugent into a ghost hunt.

Walter Guthrie drew everyone's attention when he suddenly declared, "Gentlemen, do you realize this leaves our town without a lawman?"

All eyes turned to John Stranger.

Putting his hand on the newcomer's arm, Sy Wheaton said, "John, all bets in town are that when you learn your identity, you'll discover you were a lawman. I know you're eager to ride out and learn who you are, but I believe I speak for all of us here in asking if you'd do everyone in Green River a great favor by taking the marshal's job until the killer is caught."

Stranger lifted his hat and wiped his hand across his brow. He was indeed eager to head for Abilene, Kansas, but his conscience would not allow him to ride off and leave these people without a marshal at such a crucial time. There were broad smiles when he agreed, and he was sworn in on the spot.

Kneeling down, he solemnly removed the marshal's badge from Lanny Hughes's shirtfront, and pulling a bandanna from his hip pocket, he wiped the badge clean and pinned it on his own shirt. A strange sensation came over him, a feeling that he had done this many times before—except it seemed that he should be pinning the badge on a vest.

Chapter Eight

Green River's new marshal rose from his chair in the law office and walked to the door, idly noting as he did that the lowering sun was about to go behind the mountain peaks to the west. The five town councilmen were present, and looking each of them in the eye, John Stranger said, "Well, gentlemen, I guess we've covered all the ground we can until the deputies have been chosen at the town meeting tonight. Then we'll need to meet with them to plan our strategy."

Stranger held the door open for the council members, and as he watched them head up the street, his attention was drawn to a Box B Ranch wagon coming into town. It pulled up in front of the office, and he felt his heart turn over when he looked into Bonnie Bodine's troubled face. He hurried to help her down from the wagon, opening his arms to her. Her brothers Frank and Earl waited discreetly in the wagon for a few moments.

"Oh, John," she gasped, trembling in his embrace, "we met some people on the road who told us about Lanny. How awful!"

"I'm just sick about Lanny's murder," John said softly, adding, "but then, none of these people have deserved to die. We've got a real maniac on the loose." Releasing

Bonnie, he called to her brothers, "Please, come inside."

She looked up at him, saying, "We learned of your appointment when we heard about Lanny's death. I'm glad our town will still be in capable hands after . . . after . . ."

"I know," he said gently.

They were all silent for a moment, and then Stranger asked, "What brings you to town? You've saved me a trip, since I was going to ride out to your ranch and tell you about . . . about what happened."

"Well," Frank said, "two boys rode out and told us about the town meeting tonight, so we decided to come in a bit early while the feed store and the lumberyard were still open. We need some supplies. Pa's not feeling up to the meeting, so Lamar stayed behind with him."

"Bonnie, Frank, and I will meet you back here after we buy our supplies." Earl started toward the door, adding, "By the way, when is Lanny's funeral?"

"There won't be any funeral," replied Stranger. "The councilmen and I decided that a funeral would only stir things up in this town even more than they are already, so we had Arnold Nugent take a coffin out to the cemetery and give Lanny a quick burial. None of us liked the idea, but we felt it was best. We'll have a memorial service for him once the killer is caught and everything's settled back to normal."

Staring at the badge on the new marshal's chest, Bonnie asked, "So you'll be staying on until the murderer is behind bars?"

"That's my plan."

"That star looks quite natural on you," Frank said as he walked toward the door. "I'm sorry you had to come by it under such terrible circumstances, but I think Sam would have been pleased to have you wearing it."

"Thanks, Frank. That means a lot to me."

Frank put his hand on Stranger's shoulder, and then

he said to his sister, "We'll come by for you as soon as we're done. We should have time to get a bite to eat before the meeting." Looking back at the marshal, he added, "Perhaps you'd like to join us, John."

"I'd like that. See you two later."

Earl and Frank left the office, and Stranger closed the door behind them. When he turned around, Bonnie stood squarely in front of him, and he took her in his arms and kissed her tenderly.

Still locked in his embrace, she asked, "Did you get your replies from the two Abilenes?"

"Yes, they came early this morning. It turns out that Fletcher was in both of them during the last few months, so I'll go to Kansas first. If no one knows me there, I'll head for Texas. I'll be on my way as soon as we stop this madman. The town will just have to find a new marshal once the immediate danger is over."

"Maybe they should just hire a temporary marshal, since you might be coming back."

He sighed. "Nothing would please me more than to be marshal of Green River with a certain blond beauty as my wife."

Smiling, Bonnie snuggled closer to him and said, "Now, just who might that be, Mr. Stranger?"

"I'll give you three clues," he said, and grinned. "I think she's the most gorgeous creature on God's green earth, she's the only female in this room, and her initials are B. B."

"I guess that narrows it down some, doesn't it?" Bonnie said, and then she kissed him warmly.

At seven o'clock that evening in the community church, the town meeting was held, with Clarence Roby presiding. After bringing the townspeople up to date on the murder of Lanny Hughes, he introduced John Stranger as Green River's interim marshal and then explained the council's proposal to appoint twenty-four men for the town's security until the killer among them was brought to justice.

The men were chosen by their fellow citizens and promptly deputized by John Stranger, who then told the new deputies that they would meet with the town council and himself as soon as the assembly was over. Ten minutes later Clarence Roby adjourned the meeting, and the people of Green River filed outside and went home.

Motioning to Bonnie before she left, Stranger led her off to a corner for a few moments of privacy. He took her hands in his and told her, "I'm going to be pretty busy, but I want you to know that I'll try to spend as much time with you as possible until I leave."

"I'm glad, darling," she whispered breathlessly. "I want every minute with you that I can have."

Peering around and seeing that no one was looking in their direction, Stranger bent down and stole a kiss.

Bonnie suddenly looked worried, and with a slight tremor in her voice she said, "John, I'm afraid. Maybe the killer will come after you because you're now wearing the marshal's badge."

Cupping her face in his hands, Stranger looked into her blue-gray eyes and said, "I doubt it, but I promise I'll be careful."

"Please be *very* careful," she said urgently. "I love you too much to lose you." Looking down at her hands, she added softly, "At least, not *that* way." She gave him a sweet, sad smile and then joined her brothers, who were waiting for her by the front door.

Stranger watched them leave, then joined the councilmen and the deputies to outline his strategy.

Laying out the plan for the men, he told them that twelve men would patrol at a time on twelve-hour shifts and that they would remain in pairs at all times—in case the killer was one of the deputies. They were to stay constantly alert and ready to defend the citizens of Green River and themselves.

"There's no telling how the killer might react now that an army of deputies has been assembled to bring him to justice," Stranger said.

"He was probably in the crowd tonight, so I'm sure he already knows," put in Jake Kidder.

"I have no doubt that he was," replied Stranger.

"You mean if it isn't Denzel Murdoch," Peter Condrey said nervously.

Stranger, his annoyance evident, merely stared at the hotel owner.

Glenn Easton, one of the deputies, turned to John Stranger and said, "Marshal, I've been thinkin'. Nobody who has seen the killer has lived to describe him, so we don't know what he looks like—but the one thing we know for sure is that he's got to be exceptionally strong, right?"

"That's right."

"Well . . . I'm wondering if the killer hasn't tipped his hand."

All eyes were on Easton as Stranger asked, "What do you mean?"

"I'm talkin' about the incident this afternoon. You know, when Frank Bodine lifted that hay wagon, so the wheel could be fixed."

The other deputies began to murmur in reaction to Easton's suggestion. It was true that Frank Bodine had come to the aid of a farmer that afternoon by lifting a corner of the loaded wagon so that the wheel could be replaced.

Stranger felt his scalp tighten. "You mean, you think the killer is Frank Bodine?"

"He could be."

Before Stranger could respond, Clarence Roby said, "There's no denying Frank's strength—and I hadn't thought of it until Glenn brought up his name, but we all know Frank and Denzel were pretty good friends. Maybe it was their common size and strength that brought them together, I don't know, but I do know for a fact that Frank gave Denzel money on several occasions when the poor fool was broke."

Another deputy said, "You just might have something there, Mr. Roby. Maybe Frank Bodine is getting revenge for Denzel."

John Stranger did not like the direction the conversation was taking. "Gentlemen," he said, looking intently at each of them, "Frank certainly doesn't seem the type of man who could murder someone in cold blood. True, he's as strong as an ox, but that doesn't make him the killer."

"I don't mean any offense, Marshal," T. E. Rockwell said somewhat sheepishly, "but is it possible that your feelings toward Bonnie could be clouding your judgment of her brother?"

Stranger sensed his temper quicken, but he masked it as best he could as he replied, "I'm human like everybody else, sir, but I would like to point out that my feelings for Bonnie Bodine do not prevent me from being aware that the first person to be brutally murdered was Sam Bodine, Frank's own brother."

His words quieted the talk against Frank for a few moments until Jake Kidder said to everyone, "Well, what about the bad blood between Frank and Sam? Remember when they both courted the same woman, who eventually married a third man and left town? Ever since then, each of them has blamed the other for losing her. Maybe Frank killed Sam—and is carrying out the murders as some macabre scheme to have his death pinned on Denzel!"

"That makes sense," Sy Wheaton said. "Frank knew Sam was first on Denzel's list, so it was easy to do him in and be rid of him. And now he's covering himself by murdering the rest of those on Denzel's list."

Speaking up against the voices quickly blending in agreement, John Stranger said sharply, "Now wait a minute, gentlemen. This reasoning seems to me a bit farfetched. Someone seeking revenge usually doesn't kill innocent people in addition to his victim, so it's mighty hard for me to believe that Frank would kill everyone else Denzel threatened in order to keep himself clear of suspicion. How many people in this valley would seriously suspect Frank of murdering his own brother? There may have been some hard feelings between Sam and him, but murdering his own brother would be going a long way to satisfy a grudge—and killing Sam wouldn't bring the woman back to Frank."

"But listen, Marshal," argued Jake, "what better suspect have we come up with? We need to—"

Stranger cut him off by saying, "Would Frank's name have come up here if he weren't so big and strong? Would you have even thought of him, Easton?"

Glenn Easton shrugged his shoulders and said weakly, "Well . . . no."

"So to be considered a suspect, a man would have to be exceptionally strong, which probably would also mean that he would be big, as well, since strength like that is usually coupled with size. I would venture to guess that there are a number of exceptionally large, strong men in the Green River Valley."

Irritation was clearly stamped on John Stranger's face. Staring at the blacksmith, he suddenly said, "How about you, Jake? Could you have lifted the hay wagon?"

Jake Kidder stiffened, and his face reddened. "Well, I don't know. I suppose maybe I could have. I—"

"Aren't you about the same size as Frank Bodine?"

Clearing his throat nervously, Jake admitted, "Well, yeah, but—"

"Was Denzel Murdoch any larger than you?"

Sweat beaded Jake's brow, and he said angrily, "Now look here, Stranger, don't go throwin' suspicion on me!"

The other men peered uncertainly at the blacksmith

as John Stranger added, "I'd say that you could have lifted that hay wagon, Jake. I'd also say that you could have snapped Lanny Hughes's neck with your bare hands—and I believe you're strong enough to have lifted Les Ames up into the noose."

"Yeah, but I ain't got a motive for killin' Sam!" he blurted. "No one in this valley except Frank was both a friend of Denzel Murdoch and had a grudge against Sam."

"Having been the friend of a dead man and being involved in a family spat doesn't make a man a murderer, Jake. But unfortunately since the only fact we have is that the killer is quite large and quite strong, suspicion is put on every big, strong man in the valley— including you and Frank Bodine."

Jake Kidder was speechless.

"But remember," Stranger reminded everyone, "that being a big, strong man doesn't make Jake or anyone else a murderer, so let's set our minds on one thing: One man among us *is* the killer, and we're going to catch him!"

Getting back to the business at hand, Stranger laid out the patrols and the shifts of the new deputies, and it was almost ten o'clock before the meeting came to an end. The men were solemn and quiet as they left the community church, and Green River's new marshal feared that in the minds of most of them, they now had two strong suspects—Frank Bodine and Jake Kidder. He knew that as soon as they talked with their friends and neighbors, it would not take long for their conclusions to spread to everyone else in the town.

Tormented about his identity and by the likelihood that somewhere a wife and family were waiting for him to return, John Stranger now had an added burden. Like it or not, he had to face the possibility that Bonnie's brother, because of his size and strength, could be the killer.

*   *   *

It was nearing midnight, and as the twelve heavily armed deputies patrolled Green River, the only light to be seen anywhere on the residential streets came from the moon and the lanterns held by the deputies. Along Main Street's business district, the streetlamps provided pools of warm yellow light every fifty feet, but there, too, all the store windows and hotel rooms were dark—except one.

Working unusually late to fill his backlog of orders, T. E. Rockwell sat at his sewing machine in the back room of his haberdashery store, his foot busily pumping the treadle. The bright light from his lamp glinted off the barrel of his new Winchester rifle leaning against the wall an arm's length away.

Above the rattle of the sewing machine, Rockwell heard a rap at the front door. Picking up his rifle, he made his way to the front of the shop and pulled back the shade that covered the door window. Two deputies, their faces illuminated by their lantern, peered at him through the glass.

Rockwell unlocked the door and opened it, saying to Tracy Downs and Clayton Saddler, "Well, I'm glad to see that our deputies are on the job."

"You're working kind of late, aren't you, Mr. Rockwell?" asked Downs.

"I'm trying to catch up on my suit orders—one of which is yours, Tracy," explained Rockwell with a smile. "Oh, by the way, I forgot to ask if you want bone or brass buttons on your vest."

Downs scratched his head. "Uh . . . I guess I'll have to think about that. Brass would fancy it up some, wouldn't it?"

"It would."

"I appreciate your asking. I'll decide and let you know as soon as possible," Downs assured the tailor.

"Okay, but don't take too long. I'd like to be able to finish it up."

"Sure thing."

Clayton Saddler started to leave, saying, "Well, we'll let you get back to work, T. E. But when you're ready to leave, we'll escort you home. What time are you planning on quitting?"

"I figure on working for about another hour," responded the tailor.

Saddler took out his pocket watch. "Okay, we'll be back here about one. Lock the door behind us, and keep that gun close by."

"Fine," Rockwell said as he nodded and closed the door, quickly locking it. He returned to his sewing machine in the back room, leaning the rifle up against the wall, and then he resumed his work. No more than three minutes had passed when he heard a light tap at the front door. Sighing at the interruption, he got up and walked to the front door.

"You've made up your mind about the buttons already, eh, Tracy?"

A slightly muffled voice said, "Yes."

"I'll bet you've decided on the brass—am I right?" Rockwell turned the lock and pulled open the door. His expression of slight annoyance turned to one of horror as he looked up and gasped, "Oh, my God, it really *is* you! How—"

T. E. Rockwell's words were cut off as a hatchet was buried deep in his chest, the force of the impact driving him backward before he flopped to the floor. The sharp blade had split his heart in two, killing him instantly.

The huge killer quickly stepped inside the shop and shut the door. A maniacal gleam was in his eyes as he pulled out a knife and in Rockwell's forehead carved the initials D. M. over the word INNOCENT.

Forty yards up the street Tracy Downs turned to Clayton Saddler and said, "Did you hear something?"

"Just our boots thumping on the boardwalk. What do you think you heard?"

Looking back in the direction from which they had come, Downs said, "Voices."

Two other deputies suddenly rounded the corner, waving to Downs and Saddler, and Saddler said, "Why, it's their voices that you heard."

Watching the two deputies approach, Downs shook his head. "Nope, it wasn't them," he concluded. Gesturing behind him, he added, "I thought I heard something from back there."

"Well, let's go check."

"It's probably my imagination, so you wait here with Babcock and Williams, and I'll just dash back myself and give a quick look." While he spoke, Tracy Downs was already in motion.

Inside Rockwell's shop, the killer wiped his knife clean on the dead tailor's shirt and pocketed it. He was about to open the door when he heard rapid footsteps coming closer. Quickly retreating to the back room, he spied the rifle and a box of .44 cartridges lying on a shelf above the workbench. Picking up the Winchester and stuffing the shells in his pocket, he then turned out the lamp on the bench and waited in the darkness.

Tracy Downs reached T. E. Rockwell's shop, exclaiming slightly in surprise at finding it dark. He rapped on the door and turned the knob, and finding the door unlocked, he rushed inside, almost tripping on the form on the floor. Holding his lantern in front of him, the deputy looked down and was horrified at the sight of Rockwell lying on the floor with a hatchet buried in his chest. He stood rooted to the spot, looking as though he were going to be sick, before he finally turned around to call out for his partner.

When Downs moved, so did the shadowy form at the rear of the shop, and the rifle butt slammed into the deputy's head, knocking him to the floor.

Clutching the rifle, the intruder cautiously opened

the door and peered up the street, relieved to see that
the deputy's partner was engaged in conversation with
two other men on patrol, and none of them were looking his way. He slipped out of the shop and into an
alleyway just beyond the store, vanishing into the
darkness.

Clayton Saddler turned and glanced down the dimly
lit street, deciding that by this time Tracy Downs should
have returned. Turning back to the other two deputies,
he said, "Excuse me, fellas, but I think Tracy's been
gone long enough. I'm going to see if something's wrong.
You two wait here." He hurried down the street, stopping abruptly at the door, slightly ajar, of T. E. Rockwell's shop. Taking a deep breath, he whipped out his
revolver and cautiously entered.

"Oh, no!" he moaned at the sight of the two bodies
on the floor. It was evident that Rockwell, the hatchet
sticking out of his chest, was dead, but he could not tell
if Downs had met the same fate.

Kneeling down, Saddler lifted the deputy's hand and
felt for his pulse. He was still alive! He looked around
the shop, determining what to do.

"First things first," he said under his breath. Standing up, he cocked his revolver and carefully checked
out both rooms. The killer had fled.

Deciding his first priority was to see that Tracy Downs
received medical attention, Saddler dashed outside and
called to the other two deputies as he ran up to them.
Excitedly telling them what had happened, he ordered,
"One of you men go to the shop and stay with the
victims, and the other go get the marshal. I'm going to
Doc's house to get help for Tracy."

Fifteen minutes later Marshal John Stranger strode
decisively into the tailor shop to assess the latest murder, arriving almost simultaneously with Walter Guthrie.

To all three deputies, the marshal said, "I want all the town councilmen here as soon as possible, and pass the word about this to all the other deputies on duty, as well."

Kneeling down, he helped the deputies carry Tracy Downs to the counter that Guthrie had chosen to use as an examining table. The injured man had regained consciousness and was moaning in pain.

"Can I question him yet, Doc?" Stranger asked.

"I'd give him a few more minutes for his head to completely clear. He's had a nasty blow, but I think he'll be all right."

Swearing softly, Stranger walked back to the body, standing over it. "What a horrible way to die," he said to Guthrie.

"The physician's eyebrows lifted. *Any* way someone's murdered is a horrible way to die, wouldn't you say?"

"Yeah. Tell me, Doc, what kind of strength would it take to be able to bury a hatchet so deeply in a man's chest like that?"

The physician shook his white mane, pulled off his glasses, and looked intently at the marshal. "It's one of those curious phenomena that madness sometimes confers upon its victims added abilities—strength being one of them. And this madman is as strong as an ox."

Within a half hour the rest of the deputies on patrol were standing outside on the boardwalk, and Jake Kidder, Peter Condrey, Sy Wheaton, and Clarence Roby had all arrived at the tailor's shop after being summoned. Each man had recoiled in horror at the sight of Rockwell's mutilated body.

The marshal saw Wheaton and Roby eye each other, then cast furtive glances at Jake Kidder. Neither man said anything, but obviously each was wondering if Jake had an alibi for the time the killing took place.

Speaking to the councilmen, Stranger said, "I'm sorry

to have pulled you from your beds, but since you're the leaders in this town, I think you should be in on everything that happens."

"You're right, John," agreed Jake Kidder.

The others all concurred, "We should be."

Stranger looked over at Tracy Downs, who was now sitting up on the counter. "Deputy," he asked, "can you tell us anything about what happened?"

"Well, sir, my partner and I had stopped in to check up on Mr. Rockwell because his shop was still lit up, even though it was going on midnight. He told us everything was fine, and we arranged to meet back here an hour later to escort him home." He paused to rub the back of his head. "Saddler and I left to continue on our patrol, but a couple of minutes later, I thought I heard voices and I came back to check. I found the door unlocked, got one look at poor Mr. Rockwell, and that's the last thing I remember till I woke up here on this counter."

"So you didn't get a look at who hit you?"

"No, sir."

Peter Condrey threw his hands into the air, practically shouting, "We *know* who the murderer is! Nobody has to get a look at him!"

"Don't start with that nonsense again, Condrey," Clarence Roby said disgustedly.

"Gentlemen, gentlemen, quarreling won't help matters," Stranger reminded them. "This is a time for unity, not dissension."

"Who's going to tell T. E.'s wife?" Condrey asked.

"I guess that's my job," answered Stranger. "If you can tell me where to find her house, I'll go get it over with."

"I can do that," replied Guthrie. "I know Agnes well—and she'll need something to calm her nerves when she learns she's a widow." He sighed and said, "I guess I'll just cover the body and have Arnold pick it up in the morning." He leaned over Rockwell's corpse and attempted to remove the hatchet from the dead man's chest, but it would not budge.

"Here, Doc," said Stranger. "Let me do it."

"I guess you'd better." Straightening up, the physician took a length of cloth and covered the tailor's lower body, then left to break the sad news to Agnes Rockwell.

It took several moments for Stranger to work the hatchet loose. When it came free, the marshal wrapped it in a piece of pattern paper he found on Rockwell's workbench and placed it under his arm. He pulled the cloth up over the rest of the dead man's body.

Solemnly the four members of the council prepared to leave. Stranger said, "Let me tell some of those deputies out there to escort you men home."

"It won't be necessary for me," said Jake Kidder. "Looks like the only ones the killer's after are the men Denzel named. I'm not on the list, so I'm not afraid to walk home alone."

Sy Wheaton and Clarence Roby expressed the same feelings, but Peter Condrey said with quivering lips, "I *am* on the list. I want protection back to the hotel."

"Well, I guess you three can go with him," Stranger said to Saddler, Babcock, and Williams. "Since you were all together when the killer struck, you're all in the clear."

"Every one of the deputies is, John," Jake Kidder pointed out. "Since they were patrolling in pairs, they'd sure as shootin' know if one of them was missin' when T. E. got it, and nobody's hollered that one man among them was missin'."

"You're absolutely right, Jake," Stranger agreed. Turning back to the three deputies, he said, "You men can go ahead and escort Mr. Condrey to his hotel. And you other men," he added, speaking to the other council members, "we should meet again in the morning to discuss matters further."

Bidding each other good-night, the councilmen all went back to their homes, and the other deputies went back to their patrols.

Saddler, Babcock, and Williams escorted the hotel owner out of the shop, one man on each arm and the other behind him, but their presence did little to comfort him. Condrey was nearly in a state of frenzy.

Dripping with sweat by the time he and the deputies arrived at the door of his suite in the hotel, Peter Condrey closed the door behind him and leaned against it, trying to bring his irregular breathing under control.

"I've got to get away!" he gasped aloud. "If I stay in this town, I'm a dead man!"

Panicky, irrational, and fearing for his life, he packed a small bag and left the hotel through a back door, running to the stable for his horse. He had not wanted to disturb Seth Varney, but it was too dark to find his saddle and bridle in the barn, so racing around to Varney's small house next to the corral, Condrey banged loudly on his door to awaken him.

Himself on Denzel's list for being one of the jurors, Varney's voice called cautiously from behind the door, asking the intruder to identify himself. When he was sure it was really Peter Condrey, he opened the door with a gun in one hand and a lantern in the other.

"What do you want?" grunted the hostler.

"I want my horse," demanded Condrey. "I'm leaving here right now!"

"Has something else happened?"

"Yes. The killer put a hatchet in T. E.'s chest. He's dead!"

"Oh, my God!" Varney gasped, terror in his eyes.

He started to slam the door, but Condrey begged him, "Please! You've got to help me!"

Reluctantly he threw a coat over his nightshirt and helped Peter Condrey saddle up his horse. Then as fast as his legs would carry him, he dashed back to his house and bolted the door.

Condrey tied his small bag to his saddle and swung onto his gelding, and so great was his fear that he gave no thought to which way the horse was headed when it left the stable. His only plan was to ride out of Green River as fast as the animal would carry him.

The horse had chosen to head back toward the center of town rather than the outskirts, and as Condrey rode past the Utah Hotel at a full gallop, he gave his establishment a quick glance, wondering if he could ever return to it again. At that point he did not care; his mind was completely preoccupied with getting away from the ghost of Denzel Murdoch.

As Condrey neared the other end of town, a huge figure emerged from the shadows some thirty yards ahead and stepped into a circle of yellow light cast by a streetlight. Condrey's horse whinnied in fright and began to pull up, fighting the bit, and the hotel owner felt his throat constrict in terror.

Now standing squarely in the center of the street, the man had a rifle in his hands, and he was drawing a bead directly on Peter Condrey.

Condrey desperately tried to spur his horse on, shrieking at the form that loomed threatening and venomous, "Please, Denzel, don't shoot me! I'm sorry we hung you! Please, Denzel! Don't—"

The crack of the rifle split the night, its muzzle blossoming orange against the surrounding gloom. Peter Condrey grunted as the bullet struck him, and he peeled from the saddle, hitting the ground hard as his horse galloped away in fright. The vengeful killer then vanished as quickly as he had appeared.

Immediately lights appeared in the windows of nearby houses, and deputies ran toward the sound of the shot. John Stranger raced out of T. E. Rockwell's shop and, determining the direction of the shot, raced toward the scene.

When he arrived, several deputies holding lanterns stood around the inert form of Peter Condrey, keeping the steadily increasing crowd of onlookers back.

Stranger pushed his way past the gathering crowd and knelt beside Condrey, who was still breathing. The wounded man looked up and tried to speak to the marshal, but no voice issued from his throat.

Pulling open Condrey's shirt, Stranger took one look at the wound and said to the deputies, "Let's get him to the doc's."

Carrying the victim as gently as they could, the deputies and Stranger reached Guthrie's house as fast as they could and, pounding on the door, woke the physician from a sound sleep.

"Not another one!" the elderly doctor exclaimed upon opening the front door. "Quick, get him onto the examining table in the back." Guthrie tapped one of the deputies on the shoulder. "Go down that hallway and knock on the last door. Tell Bertha Nash I need her help to remove a bullet."

After carrying the victim to the surgery, Stranger walked the deputies back to the front door and told them, "I want you men to keep a sharp eye on the town. It seems that our killer is escalating matters—and two murders in one night is as many as we're going to give him the chance to commit."

When the men had gone, the marshal hurried back to the surgery. He looked down at the patient, who was somewhat dazed but conscious, not yet having been administered the ether.

Looking up at Stranger with glassy eyes, the wounded man took hold of his arm and in a gasping voice stammered, "John! John! It . . . it was Denzel who . . . shot me! I saw him! It . . . was Denzel!"

"Did you see his face, Pete?" asked Stranger.

Condrey ran his tongue over his dry lips and replied weakly, "Yes . . . not . . . not real clear . . . but I saw him by the . . . streetlight. John . . . it . . . was Denzel!"

"Pete," Stranger said, his voice tight, "dead men don't climb out of graves, and ghosts don't fire rifles."

Nobody noticed that Henry Yeager and two of his close friends had walked into the house and were standing near the open clinic door. They were listening intently to what Peter Condrey was saying.

"John . . . he was big, real big. If . . . if I hadn't seen the face . . . I'd . . . I'd say it was . . . Frank Bodine . . . or maybe Jake Kidder. But . . . I *did* see it clear enough, John. It . . . was Denzel, I tell you! It was Denzel!"

Bertha Nash finally came wheeling into the room, and Guthrie looked at her, slightly annoyed. "Well, Bertha, at last. Let's proceed." Looking at the lawman, he added, "You'll have to stand back now, John. We've got to give him the anesthesia and dig that bullet out."

Stranger nodded and took two steps back.

Suddenly Peter Condrey coughed, gasped, and choked. Then his body jerked briefly in spasm and went still.

Sighing deeply, Walter Guthrie looked momentarily at the scalpel in his hand. It had not yet touched flesh, and he laid it on the instrument table. Confirming what he already knew, he tested for a pulse on both Condrey's wrist and neck. Then the physician said quietly, "He's dead. The bullet did too much damage."

As Guthrie drew a sheet over the lifeless body, Bertha looked at the covered form and commented, "Well, Denzel, I guess you can chalk off another one."

The physician and the marshal looked at each other. Both men knew that only by catching the real killer could they otherwise convince those who believed a ghost was responsible.

Bidding Guthrie and Bertha good-night, John Stranger rounded up his deputies and left the house. He decided he would question Jake Kidder and Frank Bodine to see if they could establish alibis. Once he had talked to them, he would act accordingly.

First going to Jake Kidder's house, Stranger found him awake and began questioning him.

"Where were you at the time of Pete's murder?"

"I was on my way home from Rockwell's shop. I heard a shot, but I was too weary to go and investigate, knowing I would learn what it was in the morning." When Stranger told him of Peter Condrey's last words, Jake bristled and said, "Marshal, I'm no killer. I don't even own a rifle."

"Can you prove you were on your way home, Jake? Was anyone with you when the shot rang out?"

The huge, muscular man shook his head. "Nope. I was alone, and as far as I know, no one saw me."

"Not owning a rifle doesn't mean you couldn't make use of one, Jake. It's too bad there's no way to corroborate your story, 'cause it may well make things difficult for you before this is over. As you know, everyone in this town is scared. Because of your size and strength, you're already considered a suspect, and this situation is going to make it even stickier." He paused and stared at the blacksmith before saying, "But let's get back to your alibi. Where were you when Rockwell was killed earlier this evening? And what about when Lanny was murdered?"

Stranger interrogated Jake closely about where he was during each of the murders. With each one, the blacksmith either did not remember or had no clear alibi.

Sighing, Stranger said, "As bad as this may look to others, there's one definite thing in your favor. I can't think of any motive you might have for killing *any* of them, much less all of them."

"You're right. I have no motive." The big man looked Stranger square in the eye. "Tell me, do you think I'm the killer, John?"

The answer was quick and emphatic. "No, I don't."

"What about Frank Bodine?" Jake demanded.

"I'll be putting the same questions to him, don't you worry. But I don't think it's Frank Bodine, either. However, as marshal of this town, I have to operate by certain rules, and I have to investigate every possible lead."

"What are you going to do about me?"

"Nothing for the time being. Like I said, your being big and strong and lacking an alibi doesn't incriminate you. This may hurt your business somewhat until you're cleared, but you'll just have to live with that."

Jake nodded solemnly.

Stranger then bade him good-night and headed for the hotel.

Chapter Nine

As soon as dawn broke, John Stranger rode out to the Box B Ranch, arriving half an hour later. He had barely dismounted when Bonnie Bodine rushed out of her house to meet him and threw her arms around him, kissing him warmly. Releasing him, her smile quickly faded as, tilting her head and looking carefully at him, she realized how somber his expression was. Throwing a quick, worried glance at her father and brothers standing behind her on the porch, she asked, "What's wrong, John?"

Wearily he replied, "I'm afraid there's been another murder—actually two of them—in the last few hours."

"Oh, no!" Bonnie exclaimed, her hand going to her mouth.

"Who?" Thomas Bodine demanded to know.

"T. E. Rockwell was killed shortly after midnight, and then Peter Condrey was shot soon thereafter. I suspect poor Condrey was trying to leave town; I guess he would have been a whole lot better off if he had just locked himself in his room."

Stranger then told them what Peter Condrey's last words had been. Frank's face tensed as the marshal admitted that in the minds of Green River's frightened populace, he and Jake Kidder would be the two prime suspects.

Thomas Bodine's husky neck reddened, and he blurted, "Frank's being a murder suspect is preposterous!"

"It certainly is, John," Bonnie said fiercely. "You don't believe Frank could have killed any of those people, do you?"

"I know how you all feel, and I completely agree with you," John assured the family. "But surely you understand how the people of the town can come to such a conclusion, knowing the killer is a man of great strength —as are Frank and Jake."

Frank shook his head and said angrily, "Guess I didn't help myself any by hoisting that hay wagon for Lloyd Baker, did I?"

"It was a nice gesture, but it sure came at the wrong time." Stranger pushed his hat back on his head and said, "I hate to have to do this, Frank, but as Green River's marshal, I must ask you where you were last night between midnight and two o'clock in the morning."

"In my bed asleep."

"Can any of the family attest to that for you?"

The Bodines looked at each other blankly, shrugging their shoulders.

Frank replied, "We all sleep in different rooms, John. Pa went to bed about nine-thirty, and the rest of us did likewise about half an hour later."

Stranger removed his hat, ran his fingers through his hair, and looked down at the ground.

"I know what you're thinking, John," said Frank, "so I'll answer your question for you. Yes, it would have been possible for me to have crawled out my window and ridden to town in time to commit both murders. But I swear to you, I didn't do it."

A strange look suddenly appeared on Frank's face. "John, do you realize the implications of this? If I were guilty of killing these two men, that means I'm also guilty of killing Sam."

"That's what it would mean," agreed Stranger.

Sadness was in the younger's man's eyes. "John, you may not be aware of it, but Sam and I had some differences between us. We—"

"I know about it, Frank. There's talk in town that because Sam caused you to lose that woman, you were angry enough to kill him for it, using the other deaths as a cover."

Frank punched his fist into his palm and swore under his breath while his brothers tried to calm him.

"John, this is terrible," Bonnie said, her eyes showing her distress.

"I might just as well tell you the rest of it," said John. "They're also saying that maybe Frank isn't using the other deaths as a cover, but that he's also avenging Denzel's death because the two of them were friends."

"Both of those charges are absolutely absurd!" Frank shouted, angered and hurt. "I would never have killed Sam over a woman—or anything else, for that matter. He was my brother. I loved him. And as for my friendship with Denzel, well, I felt sorry for him, because even though he was a bit slow-minded, he was basically a very generous and kindhearted young man. And granted, what happened to him was horrible—but it certainly didn't turn me into a killer."

"I believe you," John told him. "Unfortunately people are petrified of their own shadows right now. They're willing to grasp at any straw, no matter how thin, since any logical solution is better than a ghost who's seeking vengeance. And their fear coupled with Condrey's last words have made you a prime suspect. I'm afraid you'll just have to bear that cross until the real killer is caught."

Laying her hand on the marshal's arm, Bonnie asked, "What are you going to do? You're not going to arrest Frank, are you?"

"No," John assured her. "Just as with Jake, there's no incriminating evidence to warrant an arrest. Let's just pray that we can catch the real madman so the innocent won't suffer."

As John Stranger rode back to Green River, he reviewed all the recent events. He found it impossible to believe that either Frank Bodine or Jake Kidder could be killers, and he certainly knew that Denzel Murdoch had not risen from the grave. He was sure the truth was right in front of him, if only he could see it.

Recalling Bertha Nash's words about Denzel's chalking off another one, the marshal recited the names of the surviving men on Denzel's list of enemies: "Seth Varney. Donald Oliver. Charles Mannis." Looking grimly determined, he said to himself, "Gentlemen, I'm going to see to it that you are not added to that madman's scorecard."

Trotting along the main thoroughfare, Stranger glanced farther up the street and noticed Seth Varney going into Walter Guthrie's house. He seemed to be quite pale, and he was holding up his left hand, which was wrapped in a cloth. Clucking to his horse, the marshal rode over to Guthrie's house and dismounted, tying his gelding to the hitch rail and entering the front door a few minutes after Varney. He could hear Guthrie and the hostler talking in the examining room, so he rapped on the door. The physician called out to come in, and Stranger then asked what had happened to Varney's hand.

"Oh, it was real stupid of me. I cut it on a piece of baling wire."

Stranger breathed a sigh. "I guess I'm as spooked as everyone else," he confessed. "For a moment I thought maybe you had had a run-in with our mysterious avenger."

Laughing nervously, Varney said, "Please! I'm trying

to think about the situation only every *other* waking moment of the day." He grew serious and said, "Actually, John, I had breakfast earlier with Charlie Mannis and Don Oliver, and we all agreed that we needed to talk with you about how to protect ourselves from this maniac."

"That suits me," Stranger said. "Why don't you come over to my office when Doc's finished with you?" Looking at the elderly physician, he asked, "How long will it take, Doc?"

Doc Guthrie had unwrapped the cloth and examined the wound. "Actually, this isn't too bad, and if you wouldn't mind, Seth, I'd like to look in on another patient before I start on you. There's a young girl back in the ward who should be waking up from the anesthesia just about now, and I'd like to be there when she opens her eyes so she won't be so scared. It should only be about ten minutes or so. The bleeding's stopped from your cut, so just keep it elevated till I get back, and it'll be fine."

"Well, then," the marshal said, "as long as you're going to be here for a while, Seth, why don't I just run and get Charlie and Don, and we can figure something out right now. We can all be back in a few minutes."

"Makes sense to me."

Inside of ten minutes Stranger returned with Mannis and Oliver, and while Doc Guthrie prepared to treat Seth Varney's cut, the men discussed their options.

Doc Guthrie removed the cloth again and, eyeing the cut, said, "Sit over here in this chair, Seth. This'll be an easy one to fix up."

The marshal said, "Will you need Bertha to help, Doc? I can go look for her."

"No need, son," the physician assured him. "Besides, she's resting in her room, I believe. I think all the excitement of last night must have caught up with her."

Becoming very quiet, the marshal was lost in thought for a long time. Finally he looked up and announced loudly and dramatically, "I've come up with an idea to outwit the killer and catch him red-handed."

The three men gaped at him, astonished, and then they all began asking questions at once.

Holding up his hand, the lawman explained, "If you three men are willing, tonight I'll send you to an old abandoned farmhouse that I've seen a few miles south of town. You'll have an escort of deputies. I'll then let it be known around town that the three of you are being kept in the jail for protection—and I'll make sure that both Frank Bodine and Jake Kidder learn of it. The murderer seems very eager to get his killing done with, so he just might bite and come to the jail to get his last three victims all at once. My deputies and I will be waiting for him."

"I like the idea, John," Charlie Mannis declared. "I'll go along with it."

The other two men concurred.

"Doc," John said, "I want you to keep what you've just heard strictly to yourself. And as a precaution, I won't inform any of the deputies of the plan until it's time to execute it. That way the killer won't have any way of learning what's really being done."

"Of course, John. You can count on my discretion."

When Seth's hand was stitched and bandaged, Guthrie said, "Now, I want to see you again in two days."

"I gotta tell you, Doc, I feel a lot more confident about being able to keep that appointment now that John's worked out this plan."

His hand on Varney's shoulder, Stranger walked him to the door of the clinic with Oliver and Mannis right behind them. When the three intended victims were ready to leave, the marshal said, "Gentlemen, wait until it's completely dark, around nine o'clock, and then meet me by the gallows behind the jail. And make sure no one sees you come."

The trio agreed. When they were gone, the marshal turned to the physician and said, "I've got things to do. See you later."

"Watch yourself, son," cautioned Guthrie. "With that badge on your chest, that madman might just look upon you as a threat and decide to remove you from the picture."

Stranger grinned. "Somebody a lot prettier than you expressed the same concern, Doc. I'll be careful."

Leaving Walter Guthrie's house, the marshal mounted his horse and trotted back toward the livery, but his attention was caught by a group of men clustered in front of his office down the street. The men were obviously waiting for him to return, so he held off stabling his horse and rode up to meet them.

As he drew closer he counted eight men, and the leader of the group seemed to be Henry Yeager. Yeager's florid face looked as though it were made of hardened clay, and Stranger knew there was going to be trouble from the stocky redhead when he learned that both Jake Kidder and Frank Bodine had questionable alibis. Looking at Yeager, Stranger found it almost impossible to believe that, as many townspeople had told him, the shopkeeper had once been a warm, friendly person, and that it was only since his daughter's brutal murder that he had become so hard and bitter.

The marshal trotted his gelding up to the hitch rail and dismounted, and Yeager immediately stepped forward and demanded, "Did you talk to Kidder and Bodine?"

Swinging under the rail, Stranger looked the shorter man straight in the eye. "Yep."

"Well?"

"I'm handling it, Henry," the lawman said evenly.

"What kind of an answer is that?" Yeager snapped, and stepped closer, forcing a confrontation.

Stranger stared at each man in the crowd, then focused back on Yeager and said, "This smells like a vigilante band to me."

"It could very well be if we don't see the killer put behind bars right soon," growled Yeager. "There's gonna be an end to these bloody murders one way or the other—and if you're not willing to get it done, we will!"

Yeager's threat ignited the temper that Stranger had managed so far to control. "I'm warning you, Henry," the lawman said, glaring at the shopkeeper, "if you try taking the law into your own hands, so help me I'll throw *you* behind bars and all your friends with you! Now you back off, or you'll regret it!"

Meeting the marshal's anger with his own, his face growing even redder, Yeager stabbed a thick finger against Stranger's chest and sneered, "Are you telling us that Bodine and Kidder have alibis as to their whereabouts at the time of last night's murders? Or is it you just don't have the guts to lock them up?"

Brushing off the offending finger, the lawman admitted, "As a matter of fact, neither Bodine nor Kidder can verify where they were, but their stories sound reasonable to me, and I'm not going to jail them simply because no one can back up those stories and testify that they weren't at the scene of the crimes. Lack of a concrete alibi doesn't make either man guilty any more than does his being large and strong."

Yeager gestured at his cohorts and declared, "These men and I are only interested in stopping the killer, Stranger, and there's no question in my mind that it's either Kidder or Bodine."

"You're sure of that."

"As sure as I've ever been of anything."

Staring unwaveringly at the man, the marshal said icily, "I understand you were equally sure that it was Denzel Murdoch who killed your daughter."

A palpable silence fell over the group, and the flush on Yeager's face turned a sickly gray.

Stranger knew his words had sunk in. Squaring his shoulders, he added, "Now, like I said, I'm handling matters."

Yeager's defeat was only momentary. Thrusting his chin forward, he said stubbornly, "If you locked up both of those men and the killings stopped, you'd know you had the murderer."

Shaking his head impatiently, Stranger said, "You're not thinking clearly, Henry. Tell me, how would we determine which of the two is the guilty man? I'm sure the killer wouldn't admit to his crimes, would he?"

"Well, I don't know. We'd—"

"Should we hang them both, to be sure we've gotten the right one?"

Flustered, Yeager wiped a hand over his mouth.

"Shades of Denzel Murdoch, Henry—and I don't think this town needs any more ghosts. Now, why don't you just paddle out of here so I can do the job the town hired me to do and is paying me for, okay?"

Yeager's face reddened again, and his eyes narrowed as he shouted, "Now listen here, Stranger!"

Grabbing Yeager's arm, an elderly man in the group said, "Henry, the marshal's making sense. Let's not—"

"Shut up, Ruben!" bellowed Yeager, jerking his arm free. He stood clenching and unclenching his fists for a few moments. Then he abruptly turned to his men and growled, "Let's get out of here."

As Yeager stomped away, the marshal called after him, "Henry, I'm warning you! Let me handle matters."

Later that afternoon John Stranger looked up from his paperwork to see Bonnie Bodine ride up in front of his office and dismount. Getting up from his desk, he met her at the door with a wide smile. But his warm smile of welcome immediately turned to a look of concern as he studied her drawn, pale face. Closing the door behind her, he lifted her chin in his hand and said, "Something's wrong. What is it?"

Bonnie's gray-blue eyes misted. "Yes, you're right. I rode into town because . . . because . . ." Her chin quivered and the tears spilled from her eyes.

"Because why, darling?" Stranger asked gently.

"Because I just need you to hold me," she choked, her composure shattering.

Taking her into his arms, he stroked her hair soothingly, feeling her clinging to him with all her might as she sobbed. When her crying finally subsided, he asked, "You're upset over the accusations about Frank, aren't you?"

Nodding her head, she said, "That's part of it. Oh, John, it's so awful. Frank's terribly shaken to think that anyone could possibly believe that he might be the killer—and especially that he could have murdered his own brother."

"I have no doubt that he's innocent, honey," Stranger assured her, "and this will all be cleared up as soon as we catch the real murderer. But as I said earlier, I'm afraid that until that happens, you and your family will just have to weather the storm." He leaned back slightly to look into her face and added with a mischievous smile, "I'll gladly volunteer to hold you anytime it gets too hard for you to bear."

Bonnie managed to giggle through her tears.

Hugging the beautiful blonde to him, it occurred to Stranger that Bonnie would be the perfect means by which to let Frank know of the supposed plan to safeguard the three jurors. Although he hated the thought of not being totally honest with her, he realized that if Frank knew of the plan yet did nothing, it would clear him of any suspicion.

Still holding her close, Stranger said, "I want you to know that I'm taking definite steps to trap the killer, and we're going to have this dreadful business over with very soon." Looking deep into her eyes, he said, "I believe you told me your worry over Frank was only part of what brought you into town. What's the rest of it?"

She closed her eyes and bit down on her lower lip, wordlessly shaking her head.

"Come on now," he said softly. "What is it?"

Looking up at him, Bonnie said in a shaky voice, "Oh, John, I . . . I thought I was handling it so well . . but—"

"Handling what?"

"The possibility that you may have a wife and family waiting for you in Kansas or Texas. As my love for you grows, so does my fear that when you ride out of here, I may never see you again." Tears glistened in her eyes as she said, "I'm trying so hard to be brave, but I'm afraid my courage is waning. I . . . I'm just not sure how I'm going to cope with it if I have to give you up. I know if you're married, that's what will have to be, but . . . oh, my dearest, I love you so very much."

Gathering her tightly in his strong arms, he whispered into her ear, "And I love you, my darling. I go to sleep thinking about you, and I awake thinking about you." He sighed deeply. "I must confess that I've thought of just staying here and not pursuing my past—just taking you for my wife and living only for tomorrow. But then my conscience and my sense of right and wrong tell me that I have to learn who I am and where I belong. If I do have a wife, then I can't hurt or forsake someone who has loved me and put her trust in me."

Sniffing, Bonnie said, "I know, John, I know. And the irony is that it's because you are just this way that I love you so much." She began weeping again. "Oh, my darling, I don't know what I'll do if I lose you."

After a few minutes Bonnie's tears ceased. Releasing Stranger, she took a handkerchief out of her skirt pocket and blew her nose. "I guess I really should be getting back to the ranch," she said, wiping away her tears with her fingers. Grimacing, she added, "My goodness, I must look a sight."

"A beautiful sight," he assured her with a smile. Putting his arm around her shoulders, he kissed her cheek and propelled her toward the door, saying playfully, "Allow me to see you to your mount, ma'am."

Stranger was about to reach for the doorknob when the door opened and a thick-bodied man who looked to be in his mid-forties stepped into the office. His weathered face wore a heavy, drooping mustache, while his leather vest sported a U.S. marshal's badge.

"Howdy," Stranger said with a smile.

The husky man returned the smile and the greeting, then said, "I'm United States Marshal Claude Mosier." Nodding graciously at Bonnie, he looked back at Stranger and added, "If you're busy, I can come back later."

"No, no. I was just leaving," Bonnie put in. "I'll leave you two lawmen to your business." Patting John's arm, she said, "I'll see you tomorrow."

"You can count on it," he replied, watching as she mounted up and rode off. Then, turning to the federal man, he said, "Come in and sit down, Marshal."

Mosier removed his hat, ran a sleeve over his dusty brow, and took a chair beside the desk, watching Stranger intently as the young lawman sat in his chair.

"I've just come from Crescent Junction," Mosier said. "Marshal Keith Marksberry told me I might still be able to find a man here who was a victim of amnesia. As soon as I rode into Green River, I started asking folks on the street if that man was still around, and they informed me that the man is now their marshal. They said you're calling yourself John Stranger."

"They told you the truth," Stranger said, and smiled. "What can I do for you?"

"I need to ask if any of your memory has come back so you could tell me why were you in a gunfight with those outlaws, and if you recall anything about the bleeding one that got away."

"Not a speck of it has come back, Marshal," said Stranger morosely. "Are you on the case now?"

"Yep. Marksberry and his posse finally had to give up trying to track the man down. You know, jobs to work, families to care for—that kind of thing. So, since the money the wounded man got away with was from a federal bank, I was put on the case. I was hoping that if you were still here, you might have had your memory come back so I'd know whom I was trailing."

"I wish I could help you, Marshal," said Stranger, "but my mind is still a blank beyond the time I woke up out there in the cemetery with my side bleeding and a deep crease from a bullet on my head."

Eyeing the scar on John's temple, Mosier said, "Well, I'll just have to plod along until I find some trace of the dude so I can close in on him." He paused for a moment, then added, "Your friendly citizens also told me you're having a nasty string of murders in this town. What's going on?"

Stranger filled the federal man in on the Denzel Murdoch story, with all of its repercussions. When he had finished, Mosier stood up and donned his hat. "Well, I sure hope you catch the dirty skunk soon. And I'd best be on my way myself, since I've got my own dirty skunk who needs catching."

It was nearing four o'clock, and Stranger decided he should find out if Jake Kidder had learned about the plan to guard the jurors—and if he had not, the marshal could tell him in some way that would not seem like a deliberate ploy. Putting on his hat, he hurried out of his office and made his way over to the blacksmith shop.

The double doors of Kidder's shop were wide open, allowing the heat and smoke from the forge to dissipate, and as the marshal passed through them into the cavernous interior, he found Henry Yeager and his seven friends arrayed in a semicircle in front of the blacksmith.

Speaking angrily at the group, Kidder demanded,

"Why don't you guys get off my back? If you think I should be arrested, go tell the marshal!"

Unaware of Stranger's presence, Henry Yeager lashed back, "He hasn't got enough sense to come in out of the rain! We're tired of waiting for him to do something, and—"

"I thought I warned you to keep out of this, Yeager!" John Stranger's voice filled the large, dark room.

Yeager turned and looked at the marshal, his mouth dropping open in surprise.

"I'm telling you one last time to stay out of this," snapped Stranger.

"Something's got to be done to protect the people of this town," Yeager snapped back.

"I'm doing just that, Henry," Stranger growled. "Now, I told you earlier to let me handle it. You people hired me to enforce the law, and you may not realize it, but that's precisely what I'm doing. Apparently you've forgotten that the law of our land says that a man is innocent until proven guilty—not the other way around. So take your men and get out of here."

One of the other men spoke up and said, "I don't give a tinker's damn about your fancy philosophies, Marshal. I say that either Jake or Frank is the killer, and you should lock 'em both up to protect the three men who are left on Denzel's list."

"Yeah, Marshal," another agreed. "If you don't lock Jake and Frank up and someone else is murdered, the blood's gonna be on your hands. Now, think that one over!"

Stranger smiled to himself as he realized that Yeager and his men had inadvertently provided the perfect opportunity to tell Jake Kidder about the three jurors' being kept in the jail. Looking sternly at the man who had just spoken, he said, "I've already given you my reasons for not locking up Jake and Frank, and I'm sticking by them—but let me ease your mind about this situation. Now we know that the beast always does his killing under the cover of darkness, so tonight, I'm putting Seth Varney, Charlie Mannis, and Don Oliver in the jail for protection." Glancing at each man in the group, he asked, "Does that make you feel better?"

Henry Yeager was about to speak when a voice came from behind him, declaring, "Marshal Stranger! I've been looking all over for you!" A tall, thin, middle-aged man came hurrying forward.

Cocking his head slightly, the marshal said, "I've seen you around town, sir, but I don't know your name."

"I'm Joe Cabiness. I live on the same block where Jake lives, only my house is a bit closer to town than his."

Stranger nodded, waiting for the man to continue.

"Well, Marshal," Cabiness said eagerly, "I would have been to see you sooner, but I had to ride over to Elgin at dawn this mornin', so I just got back. But from the minute I arrived back in Green River, my ears were bein' filled with some garbage about Jake bein' suspected of doin' all this killin'."

Smiling kindly at the man, Stranger said, "I'm sure Jake appreciates your loyalty, Mr. Cabiness. But—"

"Well, it ain't Jake, Marshal!"

Henry Yeager snorted decisively and said, "I suppose you've got proof of that?"

Glaring at Yeager, Cabiness said, "You can bet your mother-in-law's corset I do!" Turning to the marshal, he stated, "The way I heard it, before Pete Condrey died, he told you the man that shot him was big like Jake or Frank but looked like Denzel. Right?"

"Yes."

"So you figure the man who shot Pete is the same man who's done all this other killin'."

Yeager looked dumbfounded and was about to speak again, but Stranger intervened and urged Cabiness to continue.

"No doubt about it," came Stranger's reply.

"Well, it ain't Jake," he repeated.

"How do you know that?" rasped Yeager.

"Let the man talk, Henry!" Stranger commanded.

"Me and my missus were up in the night because our child was sick, and we had just put out the light in our parlor and were about to head for the bedroom when that rifle shot clattered on the other side of town. We ran to the front window and looked out—not that we really expected to see somethin', mind you, but it's just what you do when somethin' like that happens. You know?"

Stranger nodded.

"Well, when we looked out, we saw Jake walkin' past our house, headin' for home, and he was lookin' over his shoulder in the direction from where the shot had come. Frances and I both got a good look at him."

Snorting again, Yeager said, "Come on, Joe. It was almost two in the morning. How can you stand there and tell us you were able to tell that, even though it was dark as pitch, you could see that it was Jake?"

Cabiness looked at Yeager smugly and crossed his arms on his chest. "Because there's a streetlamp right in front of my house—that's how, Henry."

"You'd swear in court that it was Jake?" queried Stranger.

"Frances and me both," Cabiness said, and nodded. "On a fifty-foot-high stack of Bibles!"

Jake Kidder sighed, relieved to be exonerated.

Looking sharply at Henry Yeager, John Stranger said, "It seems you and your cronies owe Mr. Kidder an apology."

Ignoring the marshal's statement, the red-faced Yeager blurted, "Then that settles it, Stranger. Now we all know who the killer is, so there'd be no way to lock up an innocent man. You'd better put Frank Bodine behind bars immediately!"

Stranger's eyes bored into Yeager. "I'm not locking Frank Bodine up, because there's not an ounce of evidence against him," he said adamantly. "How many times must I remind you that you were equally positive Denzel Murdoch was a killer?"

Henry Yeager glared at the marshal for a long moment. Then without a word he stormed out of the blacksmith shop, his friends trailing after him one by one. The last to follow was old Ruben Fryar, who gave Jake Kidder a weak apology. Then he, too, was gone.

Chapter Ten

Waiting beside the gallows at the rear of the jail at nine o'clock that night, Marshal John Stranger kept watch for the three jurors. Presently three dark forms entered the far end of the alley and moved quickly in his direction, keeping to the deeper shadows along the walls and avoiding the moonlight.

As Charles Mannis, Donald Oliver, and Seth Varney came closer, Stranger said in a half-whisper, "Evening, fellas."

"All set, Marshal?" asked Seth Varney, keeping his voice equally low.

"Primed and ready to pump," replied Stranger. "Four of the deputies will meet us here in about five minutes, although at this point, all they know is that something big is up. I'll fill them in on all the details when they get here."

"I sure hope this plan of yours works," declared Varney earnestly. "I don't think my nerves can take much more of this."

"Since our bloodthirsty friend suddenly seems to want to get his killing over and done with as soon as possible," Stranger observed, "I've got a feeling we're going to catch him tonight."

Just then, four men rounded the corner of the alley,

and as they made their way toward the gallows, the moonlight glinted off their rifle barrels. Coming up to the others and keeping their voices to a whisper, the deputies greeted the marshal and the three intended victims.

"What's the story, John?" asked Clayton Saddler, one of the deputies the marshal had chosen.

As the seven men huddled close, Stranger went over the details of his plan very carefully. When it was clear that they all understood, they left the shadows of the gallows to put the scheme into action.

Midnight came, and the moon reached its apex, growing steadily smaller in the sky. At the derelict old farmhouse the four deputies stood at their posts outside the structure, one at each corner of the house. Each deputy moved around in a small circle, periodically casting a glance toward the lighted windows and noting the whereabouts of the other two deputies visible from his position.

Time seemed to drag on interminably. Somewhere in the distance a coyote's howl rode the night air, and from amid the dense limbs of a nearby cottonwood tree, the hooting of an owl could be heard. Thick clumps of lilac bushes were scattered around the house, throwing long, monstrous-looking shadows.

Moving slowly around his post, Clayton Saddler peered into the surrounding gloom. He could not get the horrible scene at the tailor shop out of his mind, and a cold shudder ran through him. He wished this night was already past and the killer either locked up in Green River's jail or dead. Somehow the latter appealed to him more.

The deputy held his rifle in the crook of his arm and looked up at the full moon, remembering that in books he had read about werewolves, it was always a moon such as this one that set the bizarre creatures on the prowl. Shaking his head fiercely, he told himself that

werewolves were only found in fiction, and such foolish
nonsense did not really exist.

He looked over to his left, and his fellow deputy
gestured to him reassuringly. Saddler started to walk
back in the other direction, but as soon as he turned,
he heard a slight rustling sound behind him, and he
pivoted to see what it was.

Something hard suddenly slammed into the deputy's
head. Before he could even drop to the ground, strong
hands seized him and dragged him away, unconscious.

Depositing Saddler's limp form behind an enormous
clump of lilacs, the massive bear of a man grabbed the
rifle with which he had rendered Saddler unconscious
and ran along the edge of the dark shadows toward the
next guard. One by one, the man clubbed each deputy
out cold.

Stepping cautiously onto the rickety porch, the man
tiptoed to the front door, careful not to step on any
loose, squeaky boards. He turned the knob, smiling to
himself as he found the door unlocked, and pushed it
open slowly, entering a large, L-shaped room. The
room was lighted by two kerosene lanterns, one sitting
on a small table just inside the entryway and the second
around the corner out of sight. Stealthily pushing the
door closed, he saw that it was fortified with a heavy
steel bolt, and as quietly as possible, he shoved the bolt
into place. He was sure it would not be any trouble to
put bullets into his last three victims, but if somehow
one of them was momentarily able to elude him and
attempted to make a run for it, the bolt would definitely slow him down.

Gripping the rifle and ready to fire, the huge man
crept slowly forward, moving deeper into the room.
Everything was completely quiet, and he decided his
three victims were no doubt sleeping—probably in bed-
rooms off the hallway straight ahead of him.

He passed the sitting room, which jutted out to the

left, and saw the second lantern. It was propped on an old wooden crate on the other side of what appeared to be a closet whose opening was covered by a floor-length curtain. Walking by the closet, he suddenly heard the loud, distinct click of a hammer's being cocked. Spinning around, his jaw dropped as the familiar figure of Marshal John Stranger, a revolver in his hand, stepped from behind the curtain.

"It's over, Murdoch. Drop the rifle."

The huge man stared wide-eyed, first at the threatening muzzle and then at the face of the marshal. With a gasp he demanded, "How did you know?"

"I said drop the rifle!" Stranger growled.

Murdoch meekly began to lower his arm, but then he abruptly jerked the rifle up, ready to shoot.

Forced to fire, the marshal triggered his Colt .45, the bullet clipping the killer in the arm, and the man howled in pain, holding on to his bleeding arm. Then without warning the killer lashed out with his foot, kicking the gun from Stranger's hand. It skittered across the wooden floor.

Glaring furiously at the marshal, the killer stepped up to him, towering over the smaller man, and sank his powerful fingers into Stranger's shirt, throwing him into the wall.

Air gushed from the marshal's lungs, but though he was winded, his agility was intact, and he rolled his body into Murdoch's feet, toppling him over.

The huge man hit the floor with a thud, and he lay on his back and cursed.

Getting to his feet, Stranger looked around for his gun and spied it near the hallway. As he headed for it, Murdoch reached out and grabbed his ankle, and with a quick jerk the marshal was brought down. He rolled out of reach before the killer could pounce on him, but that maneuver put him farther from the revolver.

Murdoch then crawled for the gun. Stranger sprang

after him, but the killer grabbed the weapon, raising up on his knees to fire at his opponent. The lawman lunged and gripped Murdoch's right wrist just as he thumbed back the hammer, and the muzzle swerved as it fired, sending the bullet into the ceiling.

Blood was soaking the sleeve of Murdoch's upper left arm, and Stranger knew that somehow he had to hold on until the man's physical advantage was reduced by loss of blood and pain from the wound.

Swearing at Stranger, Murdoch shook his gun hand loose and snapped back the hammer again. But Stranger was in motion. He leaped to his feet and sent a kick at the gun gripped loosely in Murdoch's hand, and the revolver sailed down the dark hallway.

Furious, the huge grizzly of a man threw his weight at Stranger in an attempt to knock him to the floor, but the lawman evaded the hurling body by sidestepping, and Murdoch tumbled harmlessly onto the floor. With a roar the killer rose to his feet and charged again.

When Murdoch came at him, Stranger threw a punch with all of his weight behind it. Fist met jaw with the sound of a flat rock's being dropped into mud, and the killer dropped again to the floor. The marshal felt the shock waves from the punch all the way up his arm.

Murdoch rose to his feet. Shaking his head, he charged toward Stranger like a freight train, hissing through his clenched teeth, "I'm gonna crush you into nothing, little man!"

His fist still hurting from the last punch he had delivered, Stranger threw another one, catching the killer on the nose. It slowed the man momentarily, but Murdoch just shook his ponderous head and kept on coming.

Grabbing the lawman, Murdoch threw him across the room, and Stranger's feet tangled in the wooden crate that supported the lantern. The lantern hit the floor and shattered, splattering kerosene all over the floor and the closet curtain. Immediately the curtain caught fire, and seconds later the floor did as well.

Stranger scrambled to his feet, momentarily aware of two faces looking through a tall window just behind him. He also heard someone at the front door, trying to break it open. He knew they were the deputies, and he was relieved that Murdoch had not seriously harmed or killed them.

Realizing that he needed to act without another moment's delay, Stranger focused on the killer coming at him. He decided to use the element of surprise, and he lunged at the huge man, using his head as a battering ram and smashing his attacker in the stomach. Wind whooshed from the killer's lungs, and he staggered backward.

The room was filling with smoke as the flames enveloped the curtain and started climbing the wall. Stranger realized that if the battle did not end soon, both he and the killer would be felled by the smoke and would burn to death.

But then Murdoch closed in with wild eyes and teeth bared like fangs, lashing out furiously with both fists. Backtracking in the smoke, Stranger attempted to keep out of the way of the killer's clublike hands, and he stumbled slightly. Murdoch caught him solidly, and he felt his feet leave the floor. Then he was on his back. Just as the killer sent a vicious kick at his head, Stranger rolled from the spot and the deadly foot missed.

Holding on to the windowsill, Stranger staggered to his feet, coughing from the smoke and shaking his head to try to clear it. He caught Murdoch's reflection in the window as the killer came at him again, and he suddenly threw himself at Murdoch's feet, tripping him. The huge man's momentum carried him headlong into the window, smashing it as he crashed through it.

John Stranger leaped through the broken window and landed on top of the giant. The two men rolled in the dirt, fists swinging. Out of the corner of his eye the lawman saw one of the deputies raise his rifle to fire, but then Clayton Saddler grabbed his arm, shouting, "No! You might hit the marshal!"

Soon it was evident that the bigger man was losing strength as blood continued to pump from his wound. Stranger, bloodied and battered himself, kept throwing punches, and he caught Murdoch with a hard right to the jaw that staggered the big man. Squarely setting himself, the marshal followed the blow with a hay-maker, hurling all his weight into it, and the punch connected solidly with Murdoch's jaw. The stunned giant flopped onto his back and lay still.

Standing over him, his fists still balled and ready to continue the battle, Stranger yelled at the deputies closing in with their rifles ready. "No! I want him alive!" Gasping, he added, "He's . . . going to hang right . . . and proper!" He knelt down, and taking a pair of handcuffs from his pocket, he snapped them around the unconscious killer's wrists.

Glancing over his shoulder, Stranger saw that the old farmhouse was completely enveloped by fire. He looked up at Clayton Saddler, lit eerily by the orange glow of the flames, and said exhaustedly, "There's an extra set of handcuffs in my saddlebags. Get them for me, will you? I don't want to take any chances with him."

The deputy returned moments later, and Stranger took the cuffs from Saddler's hand and locked them just above the first pair on Murdoch's wrists.

"You were right, John," Saddler said, nodding his head. "You had it figured right."

After finding the killer's horse tied nearby, it had taken all four deputies to hoist the killer onto the ani-mal's back, belly down. As they rode away from the blazing farmhouse back toward town, Stranger told them that when they neared Green River, he would ride on ahead and summon Doc Guthrie to the jail to tend Murdoch's wound.

Arriving back at the marshal's office, Stranger marched the conscious but subdued killer into one of the two jail cells, removing the handcuffs under the watchful eyes of the four armed deputies. Doc Guthrie was then ushered into the cell, and he sat down on a chair next to the bunk where Murdoch glumly sat.

The elderly physician just stared at the killer wordlessly for a long moment before he shook his head and finally opened his medical bag and began tending Murdoch's wound.

Murdoch stared sullenly past the doctor at the lawman, finally asking, "Varney, Mannis, and Oliver weren't at the farmhouse, and they're not here in the jail, either. Where'd you put them?"

"They're with some of the other deputies at the church. Probably sleeping like babies right now. You see, I started thinking about the way Bertha had spoken so familiarly about Denzel Murdoch, and I began to wonder if she was perhaps someone other than who she claimed. Realizing that she had been in a perfect position to overhear the plan when we discussed it at the clinic, I took Doc into my confidence and changed the original plan. I had the jurors taken to the church, while I took their place at the farmhouse."

"But what if the killer had turned out to be Frank Bodine?" Clayton Saddler asked.

"I really doubted that Frank was the killer," replied Stranger, "but just in case I was wrong about my hunch concerning Bertha, I left these other deputies here at the jail. Frank, of course, had been told along with everyone else that the three intended victims would be under guard at the jail, so the deputies were ready for him, if he had shown. Obviously that didn't happen."

Catching the marshal's eye, Murdoch then asked the same question he had asked earlier at the farmhouse. "How did you know?"

"It was what you said after Pete Condrey had died—how Denzel had gotten another one."

Murdoch narrowed his eyes. "So how did that tip it off?"

"For one thing, you seemed almost pleased that another man had been murdered, and for another, the way you used Denzel's name, it was so familiar, it was as if you knew him well." Peering closely at the big man, Stranger said, "You're Denzel Murdoch's father, aren't you?"

The big man looked down at his hands.

"The wheelchair was a nice touch," Stranger told the huge man. "You knew the people of this town would never suspect a crippled woman—even if she was bigger than most of the men in the valley." Pausing, the marshal looked at the man intently and said, "You're going to hang. You know that, don't you?"

"I don't care," Murdoch declared. "I'll be with my son. I'll tell you this much, I'm not a bit sorry for killing any of those men who had a hand in putting my boy to death."

"I didn't think you would be," said Stranger. Shaking his head sadly, he added, "They were part of a big mistake, but none of those men deserved what you did to them."

Clenching his teeth, Murdoch hissed, "The only thing I regret is that I didn't get Varney, Oliver, and Mannis before you caught me."

Doc Guthrie finished treating the prisoner, and he packed his instruments into his black bag. Standing up, he looked angrily at Murdoch and said, "Tell me, Bertha—or whatever your name is—"

"Manfred. My name is Manfred Murdoch."

"—were you laughing at me behind my back all these past months at what a stupid old fool I was for having shown kindness to a destitute, lonely woman and giving her a place in my house and my practice?"

Shaking his head sadly, Murdoch said, "No, Doc, I appreciated all that you did for me, and I had no intention of hurting you. In fact, I had no intention of hurting anybody other than those men who murdered my boy."

"What about the wives and children of those men you executed?" Guthrie exploded. "They never did a thing to your son, but you've unfairly made sure they're going to suffer for the rest of their lives, haven't you!"

Murdoch's face paled, and he looked at the ground, saying nothing.

"Tell me, Murdoch," the physician demanded, "I want to hear it from you. How did all this come about?"

The killer relaxed, and he seemed glad to be able to tell his story. "I owned a piece of land that I farmed—not much, just a plot of land out in the middle of nowhere, but it gave us all that we needed," he began. "Well, when Denzel reached adulthood, he started looking for more than he could get from our farm. Mind you, my wife and I knew he was a bit slow, but he still needed what every other boy or man needs, which was a decent job and a woman to care for him. My boy went from town to town, trying to find a place where he could fit in, and then he came to Green River and said he had finally found that place. He'd write us letters telling us things were going well, and then one day he even wrote and told us that he'd met a girl who liked him. Well, I couldn't have been happier. It seemed almost too good to be true."

Pausing and looking down at his hands, Murdoch sighed deeply. "The letters quit coming soon after that. We thought that maybe he was just too busy to write or something. Then one day, a relative in Provo sent us a clipping from the newspaper account of Denzel's hanging and his subsequent exoneration. It went into great detail about how he pleaded with all you people that he was innocent, and the threats he made when he realized you were going to hang him anyway."

Murdoch, tears in his eyes, looked up at Guthrie as he continued, "My wife, who had been sickly for quite a while, took to her bed when she heard what had happened. Shortly thereafter she died. So don't talk to me about hurting innocent people, Doc! My son wasn't the only one murdered by the good people of Green River!" Choking back his sobs, he said, "It was after I buried my dear wife that I decided to make my son's promises come true, and exact vengeance against all those responsible for his death. I disguised myself as a crippled woman, invented a story to explain my presence in your town, and found a job."

"Well, you certainly had me fooled," Guthrie quickly admitted.

Then he raised his bushy white eyebrows and asked, "Tell me, Murdoch, aren't you concerned about going to meet your Maker with all that blood on your hands?"

Bitterness was written on Murdoch's face. "Why should I be? Justice has been done—at least to all but three of them. I could have died happy if I'd gotten them, too."

Shaking his head, the physician declared, "You've got a peculiar sense of what justice is, and—"

Guthrie's words were interrupted by the sound of someone bursting into the office and shouting the marshal's name. Footsteps were heard running toward the cell area, and Ruben Fryar rushed into the room, his eyes wide and his face flushed. There was a fresh bruise on his left cheekbone. Gasping for breath, he looked at Stranger and said excitedly, "Marshal! You gotta get out to the Bodine ranch pronto! They're gonna hang Frank!"

Stranger's face clouded as he propelled the physician out of the cell and locked the door. "Yeager and his bunch?" he demanded of Fryar.

"Yes! We'd been over at Henry's store all evenin', and he kept stewin' about Frank bein' the killer since Jake was cleared. All of a sudden about fifteen minutes ago, Henry decided he was goin' to the Box B and see that justice was served. I . . . I didn't want to be part of no lynchin', and I told Henry we should come over here and talk to you—I knew you'd be here, with all

those horses outside and lights in the office window—
but Henry cussed and said Frank wasn't dumb enough
to try to kill Mannis, Varney, and Oliver when they was
bein' guarded in the jail. He said that since you're so
sweet on Frank's sister, you'd never do nothin' to him,
and we might just as well go hang Frank and get it over
with. I told 'em I wasn't goin', and they took off without
me."

The marshal eyed the purpling mark on Fryar's face.
"Somebody punched you, didn't he?"

The old man's bony fingers went to the bruise. Blinking, he replied, "Yeah. Henry. He was pretty mad at
me for refusin' to go along. Smacked me a good one.
That's why I been these several minutes gettin' over
here to tell you about it. Sorta knocked me cuckoo for a
little while."

John Stranger's heart was in his throat. He told five
of the deputies to go with him and the others to lock
the office and stay put. Then, not wanting to waste
even a few minutes by waiting for the deputies, he
dashed into the street and leaped onto his horse, praying
he would not reach the Box B Ranch too late.

It seemed like an eternity before he got there, but
John Stranger finally rode over the crest of the long hill
that led down to the ranch house. A group of people,
illuminated by lanterns, were standing by a cluster of
trees to one side of the house, and as his gelding
galloped across the bridge, Stranger could make out
Frank Bodine, his hands tied behind his back, seated
on a horse under a big cottonwood. Trailing down from
the tree was a thick rope, and a man mounted on a
horse beside Frank's held the other end, which had
been fashioned into a noose. Thomas Bodine and his
other two sons were being held at gunpoint by four of
Yeager's men, while another man gripped Bonnie in his
arms. Fighting the man furiously, she was struggling to

free herself and screaming at Henry Yeager, who stood behind Frank's horse with a wide leather strap in his hand.

Stranger breathed a prayer of thanks that he was not too late and, whipping out his revolver, fired it into the air, shouting, "Stop! Stop!"

At the sound of the gunfire every face turned in his direction. Thundering into the yard and reining in sharply, he slid from his horse in a cloud of dust, his Colt .45 in his hand.

"Oh, John, thank God!" Bonnie cried.

Leveling the weapon at Henry Yeager, who was about to lash the horse's rump with the leather strap, Stranger warned, "Don't do it, Henry! You've got the wrong man! I've got the real killer behind bars!"

Looking insolently at the marshal, Yeager snapped, "You'll try anything to save your sweetheart's brother, won't you? Well, it won't work. I know a ruse when I hear one." Eyeing the ominous muzzle pointed at his chest, he sniffed derisively and added, "You're outnumbered, Stranger. If you shoot me, my men will cut you down. This cold-blooded killer has gotten away with his crimes long enough, and he's going to die right now!"

"There are five deputies right behind me, so any gunplay and a lot of blood will be shed," Stranger growled. "And I'm telling you the truth about the killer. Do yourself a favor, Yeager. Drop that strap and step away from the horse."

"So you've got the killer, huh?" Yeager sneered, looking at his men, who all laughed with him. "And just who has it turned out to be, Marshal?"

"Murdoch. It was Murdoch all the time."

There was a collective gasp, and everyone looked at each other, wide-eyed.

Henry Yeager's mouth fell open. Then he swallowed hard and said, "You're lying!"

The rumble of the deputies' horses suddenly filled the air. Looking over at the mounted men bearing down on the scene, Yeager nervously licked his lips, and as the deputies reined in and leaped from their saddles, guns drawn, Stranger asked challengingly, "You think I'm lying, do you? Ask these men."

Staring at the deputies, Yeager said to one of them, "Stranger says he's got the killer locked up. Is it true?"

"It sure is."

Snorting, Yeager said, "He says it's Murdoch."

"That's right."

The shopkeeper looked at the man with bewilderment. "But how—?"

Yeager's men stood in stunned astonishment. Stranger gestured to them, ordering, "Untie Frank Bodine and get him down off that horse. The rest of you lower your guns. And you"—he pointed at the man holding Bonnie—"you release Miss Bodine immediately!"

The man did as he was told, and she dashed into the marshal's arms and pressed her face against his chest.

"I hate to think what would have happened if you hadn't come when you did," Bonnie said softly. Then she looked up at him, peering closely, and gasped, "But your face! All that blood! What happened?"

"It took me a few minutes to subdue Murdoch," he said. "But most of the blood on me is his."

Confused, Bonnie shook her head and said, "John, how could it be Murdoch? I don't understand."

"You will, honey."

Henry Yeager stepped closer to Stranger, doubt written all over his face. "Come on, John. Do you mean to tell us you fought and captured a ghost . . . and he got his blood on you?"

"Who said anything about a ghost?" asked Stranger with a mischievous glint in his eye.

Yeager's face flushed all the way to his ears. "You said you had the killer in jail, and that it's Denzel Murdoch—even though we all know that Denzel's dead," he sputtered.

"No, Henry, I didn't say it was Denzel Murdoch. I

said I had Murdoch in jail, the very one who's been murdering the men Denzel threatened. Only this Murdoch is Denzel's *father*."

"His father!" exclaimed Henry Yeager. "I guess that means he's huge, like Denzel."

"He sure is."

"Where's he been hiding?"

"At Doc Guthrie's."

"*Doc Guthrie's?*"

"Yep. You know him as Bertha Nash."

Bertha's name echoed among everyone as they looked at each other in amazement.

"You're making this up," Yeager said sharply.

One of the deputies shook his head and assured him, "No, he's not—but I don't blame you for not believing it. If I hadn't seen him with my own eyes, I might not believe the marshal either."

Stranger then told them the whole story. When he was finished, Yeager and his cohorts were stunned.

"I believe you owe the Bodines an apology," Stranger said to the seven men, all standing with their heads hanging in shame.

Thomas Bodine lashed angrily, "I think more than an apology is in order! Or do I need to remind all of you just how close you came to lynching an innocent man?"

The marshal looked at Frank and asked, "Do you want to press charges?"

The huge man sighed and shook his head. "No, John. There's been enough trouble in these parts lately. Let's just forget it."

Stranger then said to Yeager's men, "Okay, you can all leave. Henry will join you in a couple of minutes."

"A couple of minutes?" Yeager asked nervously.

Stepping close to him and speaking through clenched teeth, the marshal rasped, "Yeah. Before you go I want to give you a little something for punching poor old Ruben Fryar." His right fist shot out unexpectedly and caught the shopkeeper flush on the jaw. Yeager went down hard and lay still.

Several of Yeager's men half carried the dazed man over to his horse and lifted him onto the saddle. Making sure he was hanging on to the saddle horn, the men then mounted up along with all their cohorts and rode slowly back to Green River.

After the deputies had also mounted up and started for town, the Bodine men gathered around Stranger, shaking his hand and complimenting him on a job well done. Thomas declared, "I don't know how we'll ever be able to thank you, John."

"There's no need to," Stranger assured him with a smile. "If you were in my shoes, you would have done the same thing."

"Maybe so. But I don't know if those men would have listened to me." He clapped the lawman on the shoulder and said, "I think me and my sons have earned our rest. Good night, John. Come on, boys. Let's go inside."

As soon as they were alone, Bonnie threw her arms around John and kissed him fervently. Finally releasing him, she asked, "How about letting me clean that blood off your face?"

"It's all right, darling," he said, and kissed her lightly. "I'll get a good bath when I get back to my hotel." Then he became more serious, and he said, "First thing in the morning, I'll wire Salt Lake for a circuit judge. As soon as Manfred Murdoch's trial is over and he's hanged, as I'm sure he will be, I'll turn my badge over to the town council and ride for Kansas."

Bonnie wrapped her arms tighter around Stranger, and she clung to him almost desperately. "I love you so much, my darling. I'm not sure I'll be able to stand it when you leave."

Pulling back from her slightly, he looked into her eyes. "We both know I have to go, honey," he breathed softly.

She bit her lip and nodded wordlessly.

After he had kissed her passionately one last time, he mounted up, saying he would see her soon, and headed off.

Stepping onto the porch, Bonnie turned and watched John Stranger riding in the moonlight until he disappeared over the crest of the hill. Then she dashed through the door and ran to her room, and in the privacy of her four walls she flung herself across her bed and cried herself to sleep.

Chapter Eleven

As he journeyed back to Green River, riding by the early-morning moonlight, Marshal John Stranger felt an enormous sense of relief at having caught the mysterious killer. He had come to like the people here, and he was glad for their sakes that their horrible nightmare was over at last.

Finally reaching town, he led his gelding in a trot down the main street, dismounting in front of his office. Then he stretched and yawned, rubbing the back of his neck before he unlocked the door and went inside. Stopping short, he smiled and shook his head. The two deputies he had left behind to keep an eye on the prisoner and the office were stretched out across both sides of the desk, asleep. Tossing his hat onto the desk, he reached up to the lamp hanging in the center of the office and raised the wick, brightening the room.

The two men stirred as Stranger's boots scraped on the floor. Opening their eyes, they sat up in the chairs quickly.

"Oh, sorry, Marshal. It was so quiet around here that we just sort of dozed off," one of them admitted.

"Did you make it in time?" the other man asked as they rose to their feet and stretched.

Smiling, Stranger nodded and said, "Yes, thank goodness." He explained what had happened, and then he added, "You two can go on home now. It's almost dawn, and I don't think we'll be having any unexpected visitors tonight if we haven't had them already."

"Did you really expect trouble from anyone?"

"Well, I wasn't sure. But now that Henry Yeager and his band of vigilantes found out how taking the law into their own hands could have turned out, I'm sure everyone will be content to wait until Murdoch's sentence is carried out nice and legal. Still, it wouldn't hurt to stay alert until then. And speaking of Murdoch and trouble, did our prisoner give you any?"

"Nope," the younger deputy replied. "He got real quiet after all the rest of you left. The only thing he asked for was a sheet of paper and a pencil. He said that now that this was over, he needed to write to someone in Provo. We left a lamp burning back there for him."

The marshal nodded, then said, "Thanks for your help, gentlemen."

"What about you, Marshal? Are you going to get some rest?"

Shaking his head, Stranger said, "It's really too late to go to bed at this point. I'll just go to the hotel, take myself a good hot bath, shave, and come back here. The minute the sun is up, word will spread like wildfire that the killer has been caught, and I'll need to be here to answer everyone's questions. I'll also need to wire Salt Lake and see how soon we can get a circuit judge for Murdoch's trial, since I don't want to leave Green River until he's been hanged."

"I wish you didn't have to leave at all. I wish you could just stay on as our marshal."

"Thanks, I appreciate that." Handing the two men their hats, he insisted, "Now go on home and get some real rest."

When the two men had gone, the lawman closed the door behind them and decided to check on Murdoch. He walked to the rear of the jail and opened the door to the cells. It squeaked loudly, and Stranger winced. Walking softly toward Murdoch's cell, he suddenly stopped short and stood dumbly, his eyes glued inside the cell. Murdoch's bulky body hung motionless from a sturdy wooden beam. Using the chair to stand on, the killer had wrapped his belt around the beam, cinched it around his neck, then kicked the chair out from under his feet. It lay on its side below him, giving mute testimony to what had happened.

Running back to the office, Stranger grabbed the key to the cell and dashed back. He unlocked the cell door, pushing it open. Looking up at the dead man, his face swollen and purple and his eyes bulging grotesquely from their sockets, Stranger was reminded of the way Les Ames had looked when Murdoch had hanged him on the gallows.

Taking a pocket knife from his pocket, Stranger righted the chair, then stood on it to cut through the belt just above Manfred's head. The huge body thudded to the floor. Climbing down off the chair, the lawman turned toward the bunk for a blanket to cover the corpse, and there he saw a sheet of paper lying next to a pencil stub. Picking up the paper, he silently read the message that Manfred Murdoch had left.

I'm not sorry for killing any of the men who were responsible for putting my innocent son to death, but I deeply regret having caused pain to any other innocent people, such as the jurors' wives and children. I truly didn't wish to harm any of the people of Green River except the guilty ones.

I missed my son badly all those years we were apart, but by the time you read this, everything will be all right. My boy and I will be together again.

M. Murdoch

Stranger shook his head, almost feeling sorry for Murdoch, and covered the body. Putting out the lamp, he returned to his desk in the office and picked up his hat. Then he walked outside, locking the door. Briefly he thought about going to Arnold Nugent's funeral parlor, but then he realized that there was no need to wake the undertaker. Manfred Murdoch would keep where he was for a few more hours.

Untying the reins from the hitch rail, the lawman led his horse over to the livery stable and unsaddled it, and by the time he reached his hotel, a hint of dawn was just appearing on the horizon.

Finding the desk clerk already up and about, the marshal easily obtained his hot water for a bath. He soaked in the tub for a long while, soothing his aching, bruised body, and by the time he had shaved and combed his hair, the sun was glowing warmly in the eastern sky.

While bathing, Stranger had planned his day. He would first see to Manfred Murdoch's burial, then set things in order at the marshal's office. Finally he would have a talk with the town council about their appointing a new marshal. Then he would be free to leave for Kansas the next day.

After a quick breakfast at the nearest café the marshal went to see Arnold Nugent, informing the undertaker—who had already heard the news of Murdoch's capture—that the prisoner's body would need to be picked up from the jail cell and given a burial at Cemetery Hill.

From there, Stranger walked to Jake Kidder's house and asked the blacksmith if he would bring Sy Wheaton and Clarence Roby to the marshal's office for a meeting as soon as possible. Kidder, too, had already heard the news.

Making his way back to the main street, Stranger smiled to himself and shook his head in amazement at the speed with which the news had traveled through Green River. As he neared his office, he was not at all surprised to see a number of townspeople already congregated, waiting for him to appear, and the buzzing of their voices increased in volume when they saw him coming.

"Congratulations, Marshal!" a middle-aged man declared as Stranger walked up to the crowd. "My money was on you all the time. I knew you'd flush out that fiend."

"How soon can we have the trial, Marshal?" asked another man. "That murderer needs to hang as soon as possible so all of this can be put behind us."

After gazing at everyone in the group, Stranger looked directly at the man who had asked the question and said flatly, "He's already taken care of it."

"What do you mean?"

"He hanged himself in his cell with his belt. He did it while I was out at Thomas Bodine's ranch trying to keep Henry Yeager and his pals from hanging Frank."

Looking beyond the crowd, Stranger saw Seth Varney, Charles Mannis, and Don Oliver hurrying up the street from the direction of the church. They rushed up to him, and each man in turn grabbed the marshal's hand, pumping it and praising him for his fine work in trapping and capturing Manfred Murdoch.

Gesturing with his thumb toward the office, Varney stormed, "I'd like to go in there and tell that murderous monster just what I think of him."

"I'm afraid that won't be possible," Stranger informed him, shaking his head. "The man's dead."

He told them of Murdoch's suicide, and then he answered all the other questions put to him by the people of Green River.

The three remaining members of the town council arrived, and the people all called for the councilmen to hire John Stranger as permanent marshal. Quieting everyone down, Stranger explained, "I appreciate your vote of confidence, but I'm sure many of you have heard that I'll be leaving now. I simply have to learn my real identity, and if I find that I have a family, I won't be returning to Green River."

A loud murmur of protest rose from the crowd. Holding up his hands again for quiet, Stranger added, "I'll tell you what: If I learn that I'm unmarried, I would like nothing better than to come back and be your marshal."

The members of the council agreed then and there that they would hold the job open for Stranger until they heard from him.

The lawman then said, "I'd like to suggest that you folks hire Clayton Saddler as temporary marshal, if he's agreeable to the idea. Jake, why don't you go find him and see if he'll take the job?"

"That won't be necessary, Jake," a voice said from the back of the crowd. Pushing his way through, Clayton Saddler shook Stranger's hand, saying, "You've got yourself an interim marshal."

"Good," Stranger said with a grin. "And I hope you've got nothing planned for the next few hours, 'cause I'd like to give you an introduction to the stack of paperwork waiting on your new desk."

Saddler gave a mock groan and pushed open the door to the office.

The crowd was breaking up when Arnold Nugent arrived for the body of Manfred Murdoch. After helping the undertaker load the lifeless form into the wagon, Stranger watched it drive off toward the cemetery. He breathed a sigh of relief before going back inside the office.

It was getting on toward noon, and John Stranger was once again alone in the office, working at his desk, when he looked up and saw a man on horseback, leading another horse, ride up and stop in front of the office. The man was U.S. Marshal Claude Mosier, and the horse he was leading carried a dead man draped facedown over its back.

Standing up, Stranger walked around his desk and stepped outside, and the instant he appeared, the sorrel gelding bearing the corpse nickered loudly and bobbed its head.

Mosier dismounted and stepped up onto the boardwalk. Pushing his hat to the back of his head and stroking his thick, droopy mustache, he said, "Mornin', Mr. Stranger."

"Good morning, Marshal. Looks like you got your man."

Before Mosier could answer, the gelding nickered and bobbed its head again, stomping a foot.

Looking at the horse, Stranger laughed and said to Mosier, "This old boy acts like he knows me."

Mosier grinned. "He ought to," he said. "He's your horse."

Stranger's eyes bulged. "*My* horse?"

"Yep."

The sorrel demanded the younger lawman's attention, and John Stranger stroked the white blaze on its nose, speaking softly to the animal. Whinnying shrilly, the horse expressed its pleasure at being reunited with its long-lost master.

Mosier squinted at Stranger, a curious look on his face. "Do me a favor," he finally said. "Walk around here and take a look at the dead man's face."

As Stranger moved around the hitch rail, he said to Mosier, "So the guy who got away took my horse."

"Yeah," the federal man said, nodding. Then he repeated, "Go on. Take a gander at him."

Approaching the corpse, Stranger idly noted that the man's hair was the same color and texture as his own. Then, sinking his fingers into the thick mop of hair, he lifted the pale face. Suddenly his eyes widened and a pallor appeared on his own cheeks, while tiny needles stabbed his spine and a cold prickling sensation ran over his scalp.

Stranger caught Mosier watching his face intently.

The federal man waited a few moments, then said, "Does that face look a little familiar to you?"

Running a hand over his mouth, Stranger replied, "Yeah. He sure does."

"He's your half brother."

Still holding the head up so the face was in full view, Stranger felt his body begin to tremble. He looked at the U.S. marshal and said, "If you know that, then you also know who I am!"

Nodding and touching the shaken man's arm, Claude Mosier said, "What say we go into your office? I'll tell you all about it."

They went inside, and while Mosier pulled a chair beside the desk, Stranger eased into his own. His mind was a jumble of thoughts. Was Mosier about to tell him that he had a wife in Kansas or Texas? Would this whole nightmare climax right now and finally end? Would he have to ride to the Box B this very day and tell Bonnie good-bye forever?

Claude Mosier removed his hat and laid it on top of a stack of papers on the desk. Looking at Stranger, he said, "I know how anxious you are to learn your identity, so I won't draw this out. Your half brother's name was Harry Desmond. You had the same father but different mothers. Harry'd been running with the Curly Stoddard gang for several months, and he was wanted for robbery and murder in Texas, New Mexico, and Colorado. The gang held up the Crescent Junction bank and headed for Green River with plans to rob the bank here, too." He added wryly, "But their plans abruptly changed after the shoot-out with you in the cemetery."

"What brought on the shoot-out?" cut in Stranger. "How did I—"

"I'll tell you the whole story if you'll let me get to one thing at a time," said Mosier, raising a hand.

"Sorry. It's just that this loss of memory is about to drive me crazy."

"I understand," the federal man said sympathetically.

"Now, as I was saying, Desmond was severely wounded during the shoot-out, but he survived, and he took the money and rode south to the home of a friend about forty miles from Green River. His friend, an outlaw by the name of Jack Whitman, dug the two bullets out of Desmond and kept him at his place to recuperate."

Stranger wanted to push Mosier for some answers, but he remained silent, eagerly waiting for more of the tale.

"I tracked Desmond to Whitman's place and got the drop on him while Whitman was away. At gunpoint he told me the story. He said his half brother, John, had been hot on his trail from Abilene, Texas."

"Texas!" exclaimed Stranger. "So it's Abilene, Texas!"

"Yep. He said you were after him like a bloodhound, intending to take him back to Texas to hang."

"If I was after my own brother, he must have done something pretty bad. Did he say what it was?"

"No," replied Mosier, "and I never did find that out. Anyway, he said you had followed his trail through Crescent Junction just after the Stoddard gang had robbed the bank there, and you caught up to them as they neared Green River. The chase ended up at Cemetery Hill, and you took them on in a gun battle. There were only four of them, since one member of the gang had already taken his share and parted from them just after the Crescent Junction holdup."

Well, I'll be, Stranger said to himself. *Won't Bonnie be pleased to find out what a good detective she'd make.*

The U.S. marshal proceeded. "In short order, you cut down three of the gang members and put two bullets in Desmond. You took a bullet in your side yourself, and when you fell to the ground, sprawled between a couple of grave markers, Harry figured you were dead. Since his own horse had been shot during the fracas, Harry grabbed yours. He was about to ride off when you tried to stand up—and your dear brother took aim and fired at your head, sure that he had killed you."

"Just a fraction of an inch's difference, and he would have been right," commented the young lawman, rubbing the scar on his temple.

"Well, it was enough to make the difference between life and death," Mosier said with a grin. "Anyway, Harry's wounds weren't in any of the vital organs, and he was able to get the bleeding stopped and make it to Whitman's place."

Leaning forward, placing his elbows on the desk, John breathed, "So my name is Desmond."

"That's right," the federal man said with a nod. "There are identification papers in your saddlebags, along with a leather vest that carries a badge."

John sat up straight. "A badge?"

"Yep."

"Then I *am* a lawman!"

Before Claude Mosier could say more, John leaped up from his chair and bolted out the door, racing to the sorrel's side. Unbuckling the strap on the saddlebag with nervous fingers, his hand closed around soft leather. He whipped out the vest, and a Texas Ranger's badge glistened in the sun.

"Hey!" he exclaimed, looking at Mosier, who now stood at the hitch rail. "I'm a Texas Ranger!"

The U.S. marshal nodded silently, and John went through the other saddlebag, pulling out a leather-bound folder that contained his identification papers. Reading them hurriedly, he learned that his full name was John S. Desmond, he resided at 430 Monroe Street in Abilene, Texas, and he held the prestigious rank of captain in the Texas Rangers.

"I figure you must have taken a leave of absence from your Ranger duties to go after your brother," said Mosier. "When you reached the Texas border, you probably took off the vest. The badge would mean nothing outside of Texas, since your jurisdiction ends at the border."

"You know, you're right," John Desmond declared with a broad grin. "Somehow that's very clear to me." He sighed, adding, "I just wish everything else was. Did Harry tell you anything about my personal life? I mean about a wife or family?"

"Nothing," replied Mosier.

John nodded. "Well, I guess that means I still have to ride to Abilene to find out any more about myself."

"You could wire the marshal there and ask him. He'd probably be able to tell you."

John shook his head. "I suppose he could, but I really need to find out firsthand. No, it looks like I'll be riding to Texas as soon as I can." He paused and peered intently at Mosier, asking, "Tell me, how did my brother die?"

The federal man ran a hand over his stubbly chin and said, "Well, while he and I were talking, his friend came riding in. Harry had apparently seen him through the window, but I wasn't aware that he had returned. I'm sure my horse standing in the yard was enough to put Whitman on guard, and Harry kept talking to distract me so his old pal could get the drop on me. But that sixth sense a lawman develops saved my life, and I was able to put a slug in Whitman and put him out of commission. However, while I was doing that, your brother went for a gun he had stashed close at hand. I had to kill him."

John nodded. "And Whitman?"

"He's healing while sitting in a jail cell, and then he's going to be extradited to Texas to stand trial for murder." Shaking his head, Mosier said, "Your brother was a pretty bad hombre, John. He ran with the worst of them."

"I sure wish I knew why I was trailing him myself," mused John.

"No doubt you'll find out when you get home."

"No doubt."

"The reason I brought Harry here," said Mosier,

"was that I figured maybe if you saw him it would jog your memory. Guess it didn't work, huh?"

"Nope, I'm afraid not—but I sure am happy to find out who I am. I want to thank you for that."

"Glad I could do that much," Mosier said, and he smiled. "Well, I've got to be on my way. If it's all right with you, I'll leave your brother for you to bury."

"I'll take care of it."

"And of course, the sorrel is yours, so he stays."

Laying a hand on the horse's rump, John said, "You bet. He and I have some catching up to do."

The two lawmen shook hands, and then U.S. Marshal Claude Mosier mounted up and rode away.

Hefting the saddlebags over his shoulder, John Desmond turned to go into his office. At that moment Jake Kidder passed by, and the lawman said with elation, "Hey, Jake! I'm a Texas Ranger!"

Grinning, Kidder said, "I guess this means you know who you are. Does that also mean you won't have to leave Green River now?"

John explained everything he had learned to the blacksmith. He then looked down at the badge pinned on his shirt and, taking it off, handed it to Kidder, adding, "I'll be leaving town for Texas within a couple of hours, so I'd better return this."

"Well, in that case, I'll advise the rest of the councilmen and tell Clayton Saddler that he'll need to report to us and be sworn in as temporary marshal this afternoon." Pausing, the big blacksmith put his hand on John Desmond's shoulder and said solemnly, "I want you to promise that you'll wire me just as soon as you get to Abilene and find out if you've got a family or not."

"I promise, Jake. If there's no wife waiting there for me, I'll resign as a Texas Ranger and hurry back to Green River."

John Desmond shook hands with Jake Kidder, and then he led the horse carrying his half brother's body to the undertaker's, paying Arnold Nugent for a plain pine box and burial.

Returning to his hotel room, he packed his meager belongings and tied them behind the saddle of his sorrel. Then he stopped at the livery stable to sell his other horse to Seth Varney.

"I sure do wish you well, John," Varney said. "And I sure do hope you'll be returning."

"Thanks, Seth. I hope so, too."

When John settled in the saddle on the sorrel's back, it felt natural, and it was evident that he had ridden many a mile on the animal. As he rode it toward the edge of Green River, many of the residents waved to him from along the street, and he wondered if he would ever see them again.

Heading west across the rolling green hills, John Desmond's emotions churned like a raging river. He was thrilled to be going home finally to learn all about himself, but the joy was almost canceled out by sadness. Deeply in love with Bonnie Bodine, a coldness came over him as he realized that he might soon be seeing her for the very last time in his life.

When he reached the crest of the hill that overlooked the Box B Ranch, he reined in and stared below at the Bodine property spread out in the brilliant sunshine. He dreaded having to ride away from Bonnie, but he knew he had to. Reluctantly nudging the sorrel forward, he rode down the gentle slope toward the big ranch house, and as he crossed the bridge he saw Bonnie's father sitting on the front porch, soaking up the sun.

Thomas Bodine waved at him and turned his head toward the house, calling for Bonnie, and she came running out the door just as John rode up. Smiling at the man she loved, she stepped off the porch and said, "Oh, you've got a new horse. He's beautiful! I love the blaze on his face and the white stockings. They're perfect. Where did you get him?"

Sliding down from the saddle, John replied softly, "He's mine, honey. I mean . . . this is the horse I rode up here on from Texas."

Bonnie's eyes widened. "Texas? John, what has happened? How do you know you rode him from Texas? How—"

"Whoa!" he said, taking hold of her shoulders. "Let me first tell you a couple of things, then I'll explain it, okay? Are your brothers around?"

"No," she answered, studying his face closely. "They're riding fence all afternoon. They won't be in until sundown."

"Well, then I'll just tell you and your father, and you can pass it on to them this evening."

Thomas Bodine called from the porch, "Come on over here and sit down, John. Bonnie, you sit next to me so you won't distract him while he tells us his news."

Laughing and winking at Bonnie, John then reached into his saddlebags and pulled out the leather portfolio and his folded vest. He waited until Bonnie was seated next to her father on the porch swing, and then he settled himself in a chair opposite them. Both father and daughter looked expectantly into his eyes and waited for him to speak.

"I guess I first ought to tell you that Manfred Murdoch committed suicide last night while I was here. He hung himself in the cell with his belt."

"Saves the town the expense of having a trial," Thomas said coldly.

John nodded, and then, after taking a deep breath, he said, "This vest is mine." As he spoke he handed it to Bonnie.

Bonnie opened the vest, exposing the badge. The beautiful blonde gasped, "John! You're a Texas Ranger!"

"Yes'm. And my name is here on these identification papers."

Taking the leather folder from him, Bonnie's eyes

quickly scanned the papers. "John S. Desmond," she read aloud. "A captain with the Texas Rangers, and you live in Abilene." She drew a short breath, then said, "Before you tell us how all this came about, I have to know. . . . Are you married?"

"I don't have the answer to that yet, honey," he told her softly. "I'm afraid I still have to ride to Abilene to find out. In fact, I'm heading straight for Texas from here."

John then told them about U.S. Marshal Claude Mosier's bringing in Harry Desmond's body, giving them every detail that Mosier had given him. Finally he explained to them that the town council would hold the marshal's job open for him, if he did not have obligations elsewhere.

Rising slowly from the porch swing, Thomas Bodine stepped over to John and put his hand on his shoulder. "I just want you to know, my boy, that I hope you come back. And if you do, it will be my pleasure to have you for a son-in-law."

Standing up to shake hands, John tried to smile as he replied, "Thank you, sir. I appreciate that."

The old man headed for the door, saying over his shoulder, "I know this leave-taking is going to be quite difficult for you two, so I'll let you have it without my presence."

When Thomas was gone, Bonnie got to her feet and wrapped her arms around John, laying her head on his chest. Attempting to ward off the inevitable parting, she said past the lump in her throat, "Your middle name starts with S. I wonder what it is."

"I think I know," he said quietly.

"What?"

"Stranger."

Pulling her head back, she looked up at him and smiled. "It probably is at that." Then the smile faded away as tears filled her eyes.

She clung to John as he pulled her close and said, "If

I'm not married, I'll be back as fast as I can to make you Mrs. John Desmond, and then we can begin our new life together. If . . . if I am, I . . . think it might be best if I simply write you a letter to tell you so . . . and . . . never return."

They held each other for a long while, kissing fervently. Then to make it as painless as possible, John let go of her abruptly and hurried to the sorrel.

Swinging into the saddle, he looked tenderly at her and said, "No matter what happens, Bonnie, dearest, I will always love you. Always."

She stood there sobbing softly, unable to speak, and as he looked at her tearstained face framed by her honey-blond hair shining in the sun, he felt as though his heart were bleeding. Pulling his horse's head around, he spurred the animal into a canter and rode off, not looking back.

Chapter Twelve

Twenty long, hard days had passed by the time John Desmond reached Abilene, Texas, just before noon. Reining in his sorrel just outside of town, he removed his hat and wiped his sweaty brow with his sleeve—unable to tell whether he was perspiring so heavily from the heat or from nervousness. As he looked down the broad main street directly in front of him, his heart throbbed so hard he could feel the pulse pounding in his temples. The moment of truth was upon him.

The town looked extremely familiar as he rode slowly along the main street through the business district, and instinctively he knew he should head west for six blocks to find Monroe Street.

A cold chill suddenly slithered down his spine. He could picture what his house looked like. It was a single-story cottage, white with black shutters, and a white picket fence surrounded the yard. Growing all along the fence was a wide border of flowers.

John strained to remember more, but it would not come.

"Hey, John!" came a friendly voice. "Welcome home!"

Turning in his saddle, he saw a man standing in front of a boot shop, smiling warmly. Returning the smile, John said, "Thanks. It's nice to be back."

A young man who was sweeping the porch of the Abilene Arms Hotel paused in his work to wave at John. Then as he rode past the bank, a distinguished-looking gray-haired man called out, "Ah, John, how good to see you again. Did you get him?"

"Yes," he assured the man with a nod. "I got him."

"Good! Dead or alive?"

"Dead."

"That's for the best, after what he did. I'm glad."

John acknowledged the man's words with what he hoped was the appropriate expression and then rode on.

After a few more blocks he recognized the intersection ahead where he should turn. Sure enough, the street sign confirmed that it was Sixth Street. He rounded the corner, tipping his hat to an elderly woman who was smiling and waving a hanky at him. The sign at the next street told him it was Monroe, and he automatically knew which way to turn.

Guiding his horse at a walk along Monroe Street, he soon spotted the white cottage with the picket fence and the large flower garden. The horse picked its way closer and closer, and with each step the animal took, the harder John's heart pounded. He abruptly reined in the sorrel when he realized that behind the fence a young woman with shiny coal-black hair was kneeling, weeding in the garden. Then his horse snorted, and she raised her head. She was about a year or two younger than himself, and she was extremely beautiful.

She stood up, and their eyes locked. The small trowel she was holding slipped unnoticed from her fingers as her lips silently formed his name. Bursting into tears, she ran toward him with her arms open wide, crying, "Johnny! Oh, Johnny, dearest, you're home! You're finally home!"

Dismounting, John Desmond's heart turned to ice as she dashed through the small gate. He knew he should open his arms to her, and he did so, feeling every ounce the hypocrite. With great effort he even managed to paste a smile on his lips.

As tears trickled down her cheeks the young woman flung her arms around him, blurting, "Oh, Johnny, I'm so glad you're back! I love you, Johnny! I love you. Did you find Harry? I was so afraid he would kill you."

Glumly John told her, "Harry's dead."

The brunette pressed her head against his chest, holding him tight and saying between sobs, "I'm . . . I'm not sorry he's dead, Johnny. You . . . me . . . the whole world is better off." Looking up at him again, she smiled through quivering lips and said, "The boys are out at the Walker farm. They'll be home at suppertime. Are they ever going to be glad to see you!"

John's spirit grew even heavier as she uttered those words. With his heart aching so for Bonnie, how could he ever be a husband to a woman he did not even know? Or a father to however many boys were at the Walker farm? But he knew that somehow he must. He had to return to his role as husband and father no matter how much he wanted to go back to Bonnie, for it was he, not they, who had changed. They were innocent, and they should not be made to do without or to suffer.

The mental picture he held of Bonnie seemed to be growing dim, and he could feel her slipping away. He would never see her again . . . never hold her in his arms again. Her sweet lips would never—

"Is something wrong, Johnny?" the dark-haired woman asked, looking deep into his eyes. "There *is* something wrong," she added, concern in her voice. "I can feel it. Please tell me."

Half choking on the words, he said, "I . . . well, yes, there is something I have to tell you. Something very important."

"Well, go on," she said, studying his face with searching eyes. "Go on."

Nodding gravely, a haunted look on his face, he licked his lips and breathed, "I . . . I have amnesia."

"Amnesia?" Her hand went to her mouth and her eyes widened.

"Could we go sit down?" he suggested. "I'll tell you all about it."

They walked over to the house, and sitting in the shade of the porch, John Desmond let the words tumble off his tongue. He told her of waking up in the cemetery outside of Green River, Utah, with his memory gone, then took her through the multiple murders, the capture of Manfred Murdoch, and bringing her to the present, explained how he had learned his identity. However, in his telling, he carefully left out any mention of Bonnie Bodine.

"I don't even know why I was trailing Harry," he said, closing off his tale. "I thought the Rangers only work in Texas."

The lovely brunette began to weep again. Taking hold of his hands and looking at him through sad eyes, she said in a trembling voice, "Johnny . . . then you don't even know me? Theresa?"

His broad shoulders drooped as he breathed, "You're my wife, Theresa. But I must be honest. I don't remember either you or our boys."

"Oh, my poor Johnny. . . ." Theresa stroked his face lovingly, and she gently kissed his cheek. "No, Johnny, dear," she said softly. "I am your *sister*, and the two boys are *my* children, your nephews. Lily was your wife, and you had no children."

It took a few seconds for Theresa's words to register in John's mind. Blinking his eyes in disbelief, he said in a shaky voice, "Did I hear you right? Did you say you're my *sister*?"

"Yes, Johnny!" she said, smiling tenderly. Taking hold of his left hand, she pointed to the white mark where a ring had been. "Don't you remember? You went after our no-good half brother because he killed Lily!"

Stunned, John asked, "Why am I not wearing the ring?"

Squeezing his hand, Theresa sighed, then replied softly, "Lily and Harry were having an affair behind your back. They had a disagreement of some kind, and when Lily threatened to tell you about their affair, Harry stabbed her and ran away. Before Lily died, she admitted the truth of the affair and asked your forgiveness. You forgave her, Johnny, but because she had broken your sacred vows, you took off your wedding ring and had it buried with her. You then took a leave of absence from the Rangers and went after Harry."

John Desmond stood up and began pacing, running his fingers through his hair. He tried to sort out everything Theresa was telling him, desperately attempting to remember any of it.

Cutting in on his thoughts, Theresa said, "You mentioned that this Dr. Guthrie took care of you when you were shot. Did he say whether there's a chance that your memory will ever come back?"

"He said it could come back all at once, a little at a time, or never. But I think there's a good chance that it will, because when I rode into Abilene, I suddenly knew what street I lived on and what the house looked like."

"That's wonderful!" Theresa exclaimed. "Maybe now that you're among familiar surroundings, everything will come back to you."

He looked at her questioningly and asked, "I know this will sound foolish, but do you and your boys live with me in this house?"

Giggling, she shook her head and explained that she and her husband, Tony, lived with their sons a few doors down the street. "I've been watching over your house and tending the garden while you were away.

That's why I was here when you arrived. And I'd say it was a lucky thing that I was."

"It certainly was," John agreed with a smile, and then he suddenly put his fingertips to his temples.

"Johnny, are you all right?" asked his sister.

"I'm just a little dizzy," he said, "but you know, I think you're right about the familiar surroundings. All of a sudden I can tell you exactly how the furniture is arranged inside my house! And . . . and I know your boys' names! They're Michael and Ted! And . . . tell me, Theresa, did Lily have light brown hair and a small mole on her left cheek?"

"Yes!" Theresa shouted. "Oh, Johnny, you're going to be all right!

Throwing back his head and laughing, he said, "My darlin' little sister, when you were a kid, I used to call you Punky, didn't I?"

Theresa swatted her brother playfully. "That's *one* memory I'd just as soon you hadn't recalled." Then, laughing and crying at the same time, Theresa embraced her brother and said, "Oh, Johnny, I'm so happy that you're alive and well and that you're beginning to remember."

John took his sister's hands in his and smiled at her, then kissed her forehead. "And now, I have something else to tell you about. . . ."

It was midafternoon, and Bonnie Bodine put the blueberry pie she had made for dessert that evening into the hot oven to bake. She wiped the flour off the counter and her hands, and then she hung her apron on a peg on the back of the pantry door. Glancing at the calendar on the wall next to the pantry, she sighed as she noted that John Desmond had now been gone for forty-one days. As each day had passed, she had marked it off, and during the last week her hopes had begun to die. While no letter had come telling her he was married, neither had the man she loved returned. She had tried to convince herself that he would at least keep his word and send a letter, but doubts were insinuating themselves into her mind. She was beginning to believe that he had decided to spare her feelings, and that she would never even hear from him again.

Sighing once more, the melancholy young woman slowly walked through the house toward the front porch. As she passed through the parlor she caught her reflection in the large wall mirror, and stopping to inspect herself, she said half aloud, "Well, at least your eyes are no longer swollen from weeping all the time." But as she uttered those words, a hot lump formed in her throat and she had to fight back the tears.

Swallowing hard, Bonnie regained her composure and stepped outside. She settled into the porch swing, idly pushing it slowly with her right foot. Feeling fidgety, she stood up and walked to the end of the porch and then back again. Her pacing continued for a good five minutes.

Finally she sat down on the swing again, picking up a Montgomery Ward catalog that she had left there earlier. She slowly turned the pages, trying to distract herself, but it was no use. Her mind kept wandering.

She recalled the conversation her father and Frank had had with her the week before, when her oldest brother, attempting to be helpful, had said, "Maybe you should face the fact that you'll probably never see John again, and let some of the young men who'd be thrilled to court you have a chance to do so."

"Yeah, honey," her father had chimed in. "One of these days, a handsome knight will come riding into your life, and John Desmond will become a pleasant memory."

"Maybe someday I'll be ready for someone else, Daddy. But not yet," she had told Thomas Bodine.

Closing the catalog and gazing off into the distance, Bonnie wondered if that day would ever come. She could not imagine wanting anyone but John.

Suddenly she realized that a rider on horseback was approaching. As she squinted at the figure her heart leaped into her throat as she saw that the horse the figure rode had a white blaze on its face and four white stockings.

She jumped up from the swing and stood on the edge of the porch, her heart pounding. Then, gripping her long skirt and flying off the porch, she ran toward the rider, her long honey-blond hair blowing in the breeze.

Reining in, John Desmond leaped from his horse and took her in his arms.

"John! Oh, John!" Bonnie cried out, tears streaming down her face. "You've come back!"

"No, my darling. I've come home."

THE BADGE

Book 9
BACKLASH
by Bill Reno

At thirty-one, Wes Clarke has his life in good order. As marshal of Twin Falls, Idaho, he has the respect of his townsmen and the love of his fiancée. But his world is turned upside down with the murder of Richard DeGarmo, president of the bank and owner of over half the town's businesses. Soon Clarke finds himself at odds with DeGarmo's niece, Jeannine, an eastern pacifist who arrives in town to take over her uncle's estate.

Jeannine falls prey to Tip Ruckman, a sweet-talking crook who has designs on the fortune she inherited. She is unaware that Ruckman hired the killers who murdered her uncle, and that he plans to kill her if she won't sell him her holdings. Clarke tries to warn her about Ruckman's evil intent, but her pride causes her to turn a deaf ear to him.

Each time Clarke uses his gun to bring peace to the town, the friction with Jeannine increases. After being appointed to the town council, she agrees with Ruckman that another man should replace Clarke as marshal, someone not so trigger-happy. Ruckman says he has just the man in mind.

By the time Jeannine becomes aware of Ruckman's true intent, it is too late. She has been flung into a trap, and all of Clarke's strength and cunning is needed to rescue her—and to make her see their passion for each other.

Read BACKLASH, on sale February 1989 wherever Bantam paperbacks are sold.